THE RAPHAEL BIBLE

"In His Will is our peace."

—Dante Alighieri, *Paradiso* iii, 85

The Raphael Bible

RUMER GODDEN

A STUDIO BOOK · THE VIKING PRESS · NEW YORK

We are indebted to Vittorio Alinari of Florence for the black-and-white photographs of the Loggia paintings, and to the Scala Society, also of Florence, for the color photographs.

All rights reserved. First published in 1970 by The Viking Press, Inc., 625 Madison Avenue, New York, N.Y. 10022. SBN 670-58943-8. Library of Congress catalog card number: 70-101783. Printed in U.S.A.

Acknowledgments: WILLIAM COLLINS SONS & CO. LTD.: From *The Psalms: A New Translation.* © The Grail (England) 1963. DOUBLEDAY & CO., INC., AND DARTON, LONGMAN & TODD LTD.: Excerpts from *The Jerusalem Bible.* Copyright © 1966 by Darton, Longman & Todd Ltd. and Doubleday and Company, Inc. Used by permission of the publishers. EYRE & SPOTTISWOODE: From *The Book of Common Prayer.* The text of the 1662 *Book of Common Prayer* is Crown copyright in England, and the extracts used herein are reproduced by permission. WILLIAM MORROW & COMPANY, INC., AND HODDER AND STOUGHTON LTD.: From *The Bible as History: The Confirmation of the Book of Books* by Dr. Werner Keller, translated by William Neil. © 1956 by Werner Keller. Reprinted with the permission of the publishers. NATIONAL COUNCIL OF THE CHURCHES OF CHRIST IN THE U.S.A.: From *The Holy Bible*: Revised Standard Version. Old Testament section copyright 1952 by Division of Christian Education of the National Council of the Churches of Christ in the United States of America. New Testament section Copyright 1946 by Division of Christian Education of the National Council of the Churches of Christ in the United States of America. OXFORD UNIVERSITY PRESS: From *The Holy Bible*: Revised Version. SAINT BENEDICT'S CONVENT: From *The Monastic Diurnal.* SHEED & WARD, INC.: The Scripture quotations not otherwise identified are in the translation of Monsignor Ronald Knox. Copyright 1944, 1948, and 1950 by Sheed & Ward, Inc., New York. With the kind permission of His Eminence the Cardinal Archbishop of Westminster.

CONTENTS

The Loggia.

PREFACE

Thousands upon thousands of people visit the Museum of the Vatican City every year; they walk up the great coil of the marble staircase—or take the lift —then up more flights of steps and, usually, down the long Galleries of the Marbles, of the Tapestries, of the Maps, until they come to the Raphael *stanze,* or rooms, to marvel at the famous frescoes, the spacing and luminous quality of light that is peculiarly Raphael's; then they come out onto the Loggia to walk along it to the oddly small marble door that leads to the Sistine Chapel with its even more famous Michelangelo frescoed ceiling and his "Last Judgement" behind the altar. Thoughts, minds—and guidebooks— are so intent on these wonders that the passers-by usually get no more than a swift impression of beauty from the Loggia, of its proportions, the grace of its arches, its jewel colours; here and there a small *grottesco*[1] may catch the eye: twin unicorns drinking from fountains; three balanced acrobats; a lion with wings.

Some people pause to look down into the court of St. Damasus[2] with its guards, and its rows of waiting cars. Groups with guides crowd to the end windows from which a glimpse of the private papal apartments can be had, but of all the throngs who walk through the Loggia—perhaps in the season as many as ten thousand people a day—seldom do more than a few look up, even for a cursory glance; yet here is one of the treasures of the Vatican—a lesser one, it is true, but a treasure all the same. In this second-floor Loggia there are thirteen perfectly proportioned arches, each with a ceiling vault, and each vault is inset with four paintings: fifty-two scenes, a sequence in brilliant colours, known as the Raphael Bible.

I first saw it many years ago and do not know now what made me stop and study it, painting by painting; being no Biblical scholar, I could not, at first, relate all the story-scenes to the magnificent text from which they came. I remember wondering then how many people could, and how many ever really looked at these scenes; this neglect seemed a waste of beauty. Next time I visited the Loggia I followed the painted sequence with the text and felt, more and more, that the Loggia deserves more than casual tourist-pilgrim glances; one sunny Roman morning the thought flashed on me, Why not try to show the Raphael Bible by itself—paintings and matching narrative—in a book?

"Bible" is not, strictly, the right name for it: the

---

[1] *Grotteschi* are not grotesques but small sculptures and paintings copied from Roman antiquities found in "grottoes" or cellars underneath houses built in Renaissance times. Raphael was deeply interested in these. [2] Saint Damasus was chosen Pope in 366 and greatly increased the prestige of the Roman See. He commissioned his friend Saint Jerome to correct the Latin Bible. Saint Jerome calls him "an incomparable man."

forty-eight Old Testament scenes go from the Creation only as far as Solomon, and with erratic gaps. Nor are any of the paintings by Raphael; it even seems doubtful that he made designs for more than one or two, if any of them, yet the whole was Raphael-inspired in Raphael's unique way; he was what Berenson and other critics have called him—a superb designer—and the Loggia owes its splendour to him.

Bramante left his architectural plans for the three loggie unfinished, so that it was really Raphael who conceived the tier of three galleries opening on the court of St. Damasus; all are beautifully proportioned, but on this second-floor Loggia Raphael orchestrated, as it were, a team of artists, each of different talents, into the harmony that marks all his work; the springing grace of the arcade, the vault paintings with their almost enamel-like finish, the painted *grotteschi*, the small bas-reliefs in stucco made from the old classical mixture of lime and the whitest marble dust that was rediscovered by Raphael's chief decorator, Giovanni da Udine, blend into what the Loggia has often been called—a Renaissance dream.

There is an absurd trend these days to despise Raphael—as if genius could ever be despised. He is out of fashion, perhaps from having become too familiar from countless reproductions of his work in pictures, on calendars, and on Christmas cards, and he has been belittled as simply "a great illustrator"; it is certainly amazing how this young painter from the town of Urbino has fixed a type of figure and landscape for Old and New Testament illustrations in the minds of millions who have never seen a Raphael original. They can be seen in every form of imitation, good and bad, with characters dressed in classic Greek or Roman style quite unlike their native Palestinian clothes. Many of his figures, too, have their eyes looking up—"rolled heavenwards"—giving a look of ecstasy which in less skilled hands becomes sentimental and overdone. The Sunday picture books and illustrated Bibles, the large coloured pictures that used to be hung up in schools, are all traceable to the Raphael cartoons for the tapestries of the Sistine Chapel, and to the paintings in the Loggia. All this is true; but, to wise eyes, genius towers above familiarity and fashion, and Raphael is still what he was called in life—"a divine painter."

Really to appreciate him one must go to Rome—as to Madrid for Velázquez, Toledo for El Greco; in the Roman air, in spite of its reputed two hundred days of sirocco every year, there seems to be a relaxation, a warmth that exactly suits this painter; Rome saw his finest flowering in work of titanic space composition, rich nuances, and the lifelike soft brushwork so much more natural and human than the work of his contemporaries. This "gentle youth" loved life and took with charm and ease the stream of homage—and commissions—given to him in Rome, while for the two other giants of the High Renaissance, Leonardo da Vinci and Michelangelo, work under the popes was a struggle and frustration. They beat their great wings, eagles caged by the very nature of their genius and their own temperaments, while Raphael, the golden eagle, simply soared.

He was born in 1483 with, to paraphrase the old saying, a silver paintbrush in his mouth, being the son of Giovanni Santi or Sanzio, court painter to the Duke of Urbino. Santi was a mediocre painter, but it seems Raphael may have been apprenticed to him; though, at eleven years old, on his father's death, he was sent to Perugia to work under the strong influence of Perugino. Then, coming to Florence—chief centre of art in those days—he was drawn into the dynamic circle of Leonardo. It was in this Florentine period, between the ages of twenty-one and twenty-five, that Raphael painted the series of his first famous Madonnas, including the beautiful "Belle Jardinière." His "Self-Portrait as a Boy," a drawing now in the Ashmolean Museum at Oxford, shows Raphael with something of the serenity of these early Madonnas—the face of the Madonna del Grand Duca is his in expression; the beauty of the woman is veiled by a

Raphael's "Self-Portrait as a Boy" in the Ashmolean Museum, Oxford.

sweet mysticism just as the power of the artist-to-be is hidden in the self-portrait by dreaminess. In later portraits Raphael's face has altered: the dark eyes under fine-drawn eyebrows, the thinned cheeks emphasizing the long nose, are intent with compelling inquiry and drive, almost a fire, but they were painted after Raphael had been called to Rome.

It was probably Bramante, the great architect of St. Peter's, who brought the young painter to the notice of Pope Julius II. For Raphael, it could not have come at a more propitious time. The year was 1509; the Pope had not only razed St. Peter's and was rebuilding it, but had swept away much of the painting in the Vatican itself, and a bevy of artists had been commissioned for new work. Michelangelo, eight years older than Raphael, was beginning his work on the Sistine Chapel ceiling, and there is no doubt that, perhaps surreptitiously as the stories tell, Raphael saw the frescoes; there was an immediate and tremendous leap forward in his own genius, so much so that when, in the series of *stanze* being redecorated as Pope Julius's own apartments, the pontiff saw the result of Raphael's first commission, he decided with his usual ruthlessness to obliterate all the work done in the rooms by other artists, except one lunette by Perugino, and gave the whole commission to the rising star.

The "Madonna del Gran Duca," Pitti Palace. (Gabinetto Fotografico)

It was in these rooms that Raphael made his Roman fame. The first, the Stanza della Segnatura, was the ecclesiastical tribune, and Raphael fittingly designed the ceiling panels as four necessary qualifications for a good pope: Theology, Jurisprudence, Philosophy, and, surprisingly and pleasingly, Poetry. On the walls were the enormous frescoes "La Disputa" and "The School of Athens," both revelations of space composition. The finished room was a triumph for Raphael, but more was to come: the next room, the Stanza d'Eliodoro, has, among other frescoes, "The Deliverance of Saint Peter from Prison," the most sublime mural that Raphael ever created; it is cleverly placed over the window in the darkest part of the room so that the delivering angel seems really a shining spirit of flame and light from a celestial world.

Pope Julius died in 1513 and was succeeded by Leo X, but though the new Pope was one of the Medici, an aristocrat of intellect and culture, he had not the flair, the vision of the rougher soldier Julius. When Michelangelo was planning to make Julius's statue in front of the church of St. Petronio at Bologna, he asked whether the Pope would have a book in his left hand. "Give me a sword," said Julius; "I am no scholar"; but he had understood and had patience with the vagaries of genius, while Leo X was soon on bad terms with his two greatest artists: he grew

exasperated by Leonardo da Vinci's experiments and procrastination—"Tell me if *anything* ever gets finished," the artist himself wrote in his own notebooks —and Leonardo went back to Florence. Michelangelo, in spite of frequent flights and misunderstandings, was to live on to work under six more popes, becoming, in his turn, architect of St. Peter's, and painting his tremendous "Last Judgement" behind the altar of the Sistine Chapel, but under Leo X he grew ever more frustrated, crabbed, and quarrelsome.

The quarrels between Raphael and Michelangelo have become legendary and wildly exaggerated. It is true that in the early days the older artist wrote a letter full of bitterness in which he declared that it was Bramante and Raphael's jealousy that caused work to be stopped on the tomb Pope Julius had ordered for himself and so forced Michelangelo to leave the sculpture in which he excelled for the painting of the Sistine frescoes; but Michelangelo quarrelled with everyone, even his own pupils, even the Pope, and it is difficult to imagine the brilliantly successful Raphael as jealous.

There was, of course, rivalry, and Raphael is supposed to have persuaded Bramante to let him into the Sistine Chapel which Michelangelo had locked, not even allowing the Pope to see the frescoes before they were finished; but a better tale, the other way round, is told by Luigi Zanazzo, the Roman poet: when Raphael was painting his frescoes at the Farnesina palace for the banker Agostino Chigi, Raphael, too, would let no one in; Michelangelo disguised himself as a flower seller and slipped into the room when no one was there. He had a good look at an unfinished fresco, then, with a charcoal pencil, drew a head into it and stole away.

When Raphael came back he saw the head at once, recognized its beauty, and said it must not be erased as his indignant pupils wanted. "Such a work of art," he said, "should be preserved forever." The head can still be seen in a lunette in the Galatea room at the Farnesina and is called "the most expensive visiting card ever left."

Instinctively one likes the nonconformity, even rebelliousness, that was at the heart of Michelangelo's and Leonardo da Vinci's troubles, while feeling suspicious of the effortless, unalloyed lovcliness of Raphael, distrustful, too, of easy success—rightly distrustful. In the end, Raphael was undone by it. Pope Leo's demands on him were unremitting: when Bramante died the young man was appointed chief architect of the Vatican and St. Peter's—the huge church was still not finished; he was also made Prefect of Antiquities. So at the age of thirty-one, all the art of Rome was in his hands. There were endless painting commissions, too, not only from the Pope, but from the enormously rich Agostino Chigi for the Villa Farnesina; commissions poured in for frescoes, portraits, Madonnas, but Raphael seems to have taken them with calmness and without conceit, making no objection when the Pope called on him to advise on the Vatican's obstinately smoking chimneys or to paint a portrait of his, Leo's, pet elephant. The elephant had been sent as a present to the Pope by the King of Portugal; elephants had not been seen in Italy since the days of Hannibal, and this one used to dance to the music of pipes in the Vatican gardens, so no wonder the Pope prized it. The elephant died, but Raphael still painted the portrait; one must hope it was not in the heat of the Roman summer![3]

It must all have been more than gratifying, but no one could live long at such a pace, and the pace did not come only from painting; Raphael, in his last years, must have been the "catch" of Rome: young, handsome, rich now, with illustrious friends. Many people tried to persuade him into marriage; Cardinal Bibbiena even succeeded in betrothing him to his own niece, but Raphael made pretext after pretext to postpone the wedding; he liked his own and free amours and fell passionately in love with the beautiful dark-eyed Simona, the baker's daughter of the elegantly beautiful "La Fornarina" portrait.

[3] The portrait is lost, but a *stucchino* of an elephant is in the Loggia.

The "Madonna della Seggiola,"
Pitti Palace. (Gabinetto Fotografico)

It has often been thought that Browning, in "One Word More," invented the fancy of Raphael writing "a century of sonnets":

> . . . made and wrote them in a certain volume
> Dinted with the silver-pointed pencil
> Else he only used to draw Madonnas . . .

but Raphael wrote sonnet after sonnet to Simona.

It is interesting that the green-blue-and-gold turban of the sensuous, half-naked beauty of La Fornarina appears again as the headdress of the Madonna della Seggiola, one of Raphael's greatest compositions—and the only round one—painted on the bottom of a wine cask. He was not afraid to paint the Madonna as a woman now, but it is obvious that he never learned to say "no" either to a woman or to art; he fell into excesses just as he fell into the trap of taking too many commissions; indeed, Raphael's "workshop" became so notorious that it might seem, in his last six years, that none of the Raphaels were painted by Raphael. A great deal of the work was delegated to underlings; his head assistant, Giulio Romano, though not allowed to sign his name, painted carnations of a peculiar red brick colour as his signature, and they appear over and over again. The workshop was large and tremendously busy, but there were still to be paintings unmistakably by the master and no one else; to this last period belong the most magnificent of Raphael's Madonnas, including the Madonna with Saint Sixtus and Saint Barbara, which has been pronounced not only Raphael's greatest but the greatest Madonna in the world. It seems that not even the artist, nor his contemporaries, realized that this picture was unique; and it was sent, without particular remark, to Piacenza, to the black monks of Saint Sixtus, which is why it is called the "Sistine" or "Sixtine" Madonna—not to be confused with the Chapel in Rome. There is, too, the final wonder of the huge "Transfiguration" on which Raphael was working when he died. He lived only long enough to paint the upper half where the figure of Christ soars above the clouds.

The last of what might be called the public works of Raphael's extraordinary vitality of concept was the Loggia. It was begun in 1517 and finished in 1519 or 1520. Some of the paintings and *grotteschi* are badly damaged now; the open arcades have had to be glassed in to save the rest; the windows have shabby curtains; the court of St. Damasus is oddly shabby, too, with its old marble and dirty glass; the lower half of Giovanni da Udine's decorations have had to be covered in grilles as protection from the crowds; but the Loggia still glows as its paintings glow in their settings of lapis lazuli, amber, green, pink, and pale gold.

There are two ways of seeing the Loggia. The first is to study the individual paintings, noticing their differences, their strength or weakness, trying to attribute them to Raphael's different pupils, though this is a thorny task; no two critics have ever agreed completely on who painted what, except in the Joshua scenes, which all agree are the work of a late-comer

Raphael's "Sistine Madonna."

to the workshop, Perino del Vaga. The first vault, of "The Creation," is especially fine, and there is such beauty in the composition of "God Commands Isaac" and again in the luminous quality of "Jacob's Dream," where the angels are not ascending a ladder but a path of light, that it seems likely that these, at least, might have been from compositions by Raphael. To me, the painting that shines out is the dalliance of Isaac and Rebecca spied on by King Abimelech. Reproduced in black and white, it shows little of its quality, because it is the mysterious and fascinating painting of the back light that gives the picture such emotion; the lovers embrace in a ray of light from the setting sun while everything around is in deep shadow, even the king himself.

To study the Loggia like this, painting by painting, certainly gives insight into Raphael's methods. That his workshop was so large and busy seems to us moderns a detraction from the artist—we admire far more Michelangelo painting his great Sistine frescoes quite alone, even grinding his own colours—but Raphael's workshop was not a factory, it was a furnace of art. It seems to have been divided into two: one department for figure painting and landscape under Giulio Romano with his stormy, violent style; another for decoration under the talented Giovanni da Udine, who excelled in painting animals, birds, flowers. The Loggia was perhaps the first example in art of free teamwork; before, in the Florentine tradition, apprentices had been told to paint in a small part of a fresco or picture—a hand, a landscape-background, an animal or an angel, or the enchanting *putti* (cherubs) that embellish paintings of that time. For the Loggia, the pupils or assistants were allowed to paint whole scenes; this may have been from Raphael's known tolerance and liberality, but, far more likely, he may simply have been too busy to oversee details; he left them to Giulio Romano or Giovanni da Udine. Mere contact with Raphael seems to have been enough, however, and it is significant that after his death, when the painters dispersed, none of them reached the heights of the Loggia again.

This is why it is better to see the Loggia in the second way—as a whole; then one can see not his "school" but Raphael himself. ". . . the fact that it seems positive he did not do a brush stroke in the long series of scenes, grisailles, and *grotteschi* has nothing to do with it; without him they could never have existed, just as colour without light cannot exist."[4] These Bible story-scenes are lifted into a lofty aspiration, perhaps simply achieved by placing them in the ceiling so that one has to look up to see them. They give a curious feeling of inspiration in their frames of illusionary architecture and the delicate decoration in

[4] Alessandro Marabottini, *Raffaello* (published by Istituto Geografico de Agostini Novara).

which Giovanni da Udine excelled: medallions of angels with lions, simulated marble columns, cornices and windows above which birds fly, griffons, golden medallions on azure and emerald; these do not steal from the scenes but set them off in perfect balance. "One must remember too that they are not meant to be looked at simply as solutions of form and colour; the success of such pictures depends on how well they tell the episodes of the continued stories, make the doctrine clear."[5] Nothing could be clearer than the Loggia scenes, though their choice may be erratic, with wide gaps in time and with some of the most dramatic scenes oddly omitted:[6] scenes such as Cain and Abel, Abraham's sacrifice of Isaac, Gideon and the fleece, the story of Samson, the riddle of the honeycomb, Samuel's call—we only see Samuel as an old man anointing David. Yet the Loggia remains Raphael's Renaissance dream and is best appreciated by viewing it as a whole and by following the stories from vault to vault in a flow of great beauty.

The Loggia was painted four hundred and fifty years ago; it has been given two or three pages, a few paragraphs, sometimes only a few lines in books on the Vatican treasures, or on Raphael's art. Now, in this book, for the first time an attempt has been made to show the Loggia whole and tell its story, but to reduce eight great books of the Bible to a short text has been a more than daunting task (it can be seen from the notes what has had to be left out); only those stories that are needed to match the paintings or act as links between them are included. The stories, of course, are from the historical books, but, to give a deeper feeling of the poetry, wisdom, and beauty of the Old Testament, quotations have been added, sometimes only a line, or one verse, from the poetical and prophetical books such as the Psalms, Proverbs, Isaiah, the Song of Solomon; these quotations have been taken from the translation that seemed to offer the finest version of each: the King James Authorized Bible; the Douay; the Revised Standard; the Jerusalem Bible; the Monastic Diurnal of St. Joseph, Minnesota, U.S.A.; the Book of Common Prayer. For the text itself, the translation that seemed to lend itself best—being neither archaic nor too modern, with a splendid rhythm and flow—was the Knox. The story is told in extracts from the Old Testament, taken from Genesis; Exodus; Numbers; Deuteronomy; Joshua; the First, Second, and Third Book of Kings; the First and Second Book of Paralipomena; and from Matthew in the New Testament. Now and again, for clarity, names instead of pronouns have been used—and the names are the familiar ones that Monsignor Knox discarded when he gave Noe for

[5] From the Preface by Betty Burroughs for *The Essential Vasari* (London: Allen and Unwin). [6] See notes, page 227.

Self-portrait, a detail from "S. Luca che ritrae la Madonna." Accademia di San Luca, Rome. (Gaggiotti Roberto)

Noah, Josue for Joshua, etc. Once or twice, for continuity's sake, the order of paragraphs has been reversed.

The Raphael Bible finishes with four paintings from the New Testament: the Nativity, the Presentation in the Temple, the Baptism of Christ in the Jordan, and the Crucifixion. These are not included here as they seemed to upset the balance of the text, which ends with the chronology that, in the Bible, opens like a ray of light from the stem of Jesse, through David and Solomon, to Jesus.

Raphael died on Good Friday, April 6, 1520—his thirty-seventh birthday; he had always been delicate, and it was a wonder, a contemporary wrote, that he existed as long as he did—he was all spirit. He died from a chill, taken as he stood in one of the vast halls of the Vatican, discussing with Pope Leo the progress of St. Peter's. Vasari tells us the body was carried into the painting room where Raphael's last picture, the huge unfinished "Transfiguration," was placed at the head of the bier. It was carried, too, in the funeral procession, so that he died as he had lived, surrounded by painting. He is buried where the Kings of Italy were afterwards buried—in the Pantheon—his tomb in a small arch below an ornamental altar, and on the narrow stone coffin are his name and the words *"Ossa et ceneri,"* "bones and ashes." Every day that epitaph is contradicted.

The guidebooks tell that there are always fresh flowers on his grave; I went to see several times, and it was true. Carnations are the festival flowers of Italy, showered on the stage as tributes to singers on gala opera nights; I had brought deep red ones for Raphael and left them with the rest.

THE BEGINNING△

God, at the beginning of time, created heaven and earth. Earth was still an empty waste, and darkness hung over the deep; but already, over its waters, brooded the Spirit of God. Then God said, Let there be light; and the light began. God saw the light, and found it good, and he divided the spheres of light and darkness; the light he called Day, and the darkness Night. So evening came, and morning, and one day passed.

△ The triangle indicates a reference note–see pages 227–46.

GOD SEPARATES THE ELEMENTS△

God said, too, Let a solid vault arise amid the waters, to keep these waters apart from those; a vault by which God would separate the waters which were beneath it from the waters above it; and so it was done. This vault God called the sky. So evening came, and morning, and a second day passed.

CREATION OF THE SEA AND THE EARTH

And now God said, Let the waters below the vault collect in one place to make dry land appear. And so it was done; the dry land God called Earth, and the water, where it had collected, he called the Sea. All this God saw, and found it good. Let the earth, he said, yield grasses that grow and seed; fruit-trees too, each giving fruit of its own kind, and so propagating itself on earth. And so it was done; the earth yielded grasses that grew and seeded, each according to its kind, and trees that bore fruit, each with the power to propagate its own kind. And God saw it, and found it good. So evening came, and morning, and a third day passed.

CREATION OF THE SUN AND THE MOON△

Next, God said, Let there be luminaries in the vault of the sky, to divide the spheres of day and night; let them give portents, and be the measures of time, to mark out the day and the year; let them shine in the sky's vault, and shed light on the earth. And so it was done.

God made the two great luminaries, the greater of them to command the day, and the lesser to command the night; then he made the stars. All these he put in the vault of the sky, to shed their light on the earth, to control day and night, and divide the spheres of light and darkness. And God saw it, and found it good. So evening came, and morning, and a fourth day passed.

Wolf shall live at peace with lamb,
leopard take its ease with kid; calf and
lion and sheep in one dwelling place. . .
Cattle and bears all at pasture, their
young ones lying down together, lion
eating straw like ox. . . .
(Isaiah 11: vi—vii. Knox Bible.)

CREATION OF THE ANIMALS△

After this, God said, Let the waters produce moving things that have life in them, and winged things that fly above the earth under the sky's vault. Thus God created the huge sea-beasts, and all the different kinds of life and movement that spring from the waters, and all the different kinds of flying things; and God saw it, and found it good. He pronounced his blessing on them, Increase and multiply, and fill the waters of the sea; and let there be abundance of flying things on the earth. So evening came, and morning, and a fifth day passed. God said, too, Let the land yield all different kinds of living things, cattle and creeping things and wild beasts of every sort; and so it was done. God made every sort of wild beast, and all the different kinds of cattle and of creeping things; and God saw it, and found it good.

When I look at the heavens, the work
of Thy fingers, at the moon and the
stars, which Thou hast made.
What then is man, that Thou art
mindful of him, what the son of man
that Thou showest him regard?
Thou hast placed him hardly lower than
the Angels, Thou hast crowned him
with glory and honour; and Thou didst
set him to rule over the works of Thy
hand.
All things Thou hast laid at his feet:
sheep and oxen, all of them, and the
beasts of the field;
The birds of the air and the fishes
of the sea, whatsoever moveth in the paths
of the deep.
LORD, our LORD! how wonderful is
Thy Name over all the earth!
(Psalm 8: iv—ix. The Monastic
Diurnal, St. Joseph, Minnesota.)

And God said, Let us make man, wearing our own image and likeness; let us put him in command of the fishes in the sea, and all that flies through the air, and the cattle, and the whole earth, and all the creeping things that move on earth. So God made man in his own image, made him in the image of God. . . .

So evening came, and morning, and a sixth day passed.

By the seventh day, God had come to an end of making, and rested. . . . That is why God gave the seventh day his blessing, and hallowed it. . . .

So were heaven and earth made; heaven and earth, alike of God's fashioning. . . . Already he had planted a garden of delight . . . and here, in the middle of the garden, grew the tree of life, and the tree which brings knowledge of good and evil. . . . So the Lord God took the man [Adam] and put him in his garden of delight, to cultivate and tend it. And this was the command which the Lord God gave the man, Thou mayest eat thy fill of all the trees in the garden except the tree which brings knowledge of good and evil; if ever thou eatest of this, thy doom is death.

There be three things which are too
wonderful for me, yea, four which I
know not:
The way of an eagle in the air; the way
of a serpent upon a rock; the way of
a ship in the midst of the sea;
and the way of a man with a maid.
(Proverbs 30: xviii—xix. Authorized
Version.)

GOD PRESENTS EVE TO ADAM

But the Lord God said, It is not well that man should be without companionship; I will give him a mate of his own kind. . . . So the Lord God made Adam fall into a deep sleep, and, while he slept, took away one of his ribs, and filled its place with flesh. This rib, which he had taken out of Adam, the Lord God formed into a woman; and when he brought her to Adam, Adam said, Here, at last, is bone that comes from mine, flesh that comes from mine; it shall be called Woman, this thing that was taken out of Man.

THE SIN OF ADAM

Of all the beasts which the Lord God had made, there was none that could match the serpent in cunning. It was he who said to the woman, What is this command God has given you, not to eat the fruit of any tree in the garden? To which the woman answered, We can eat the fruit of any tree in the garden except the tree in the middle of it; it is this God has forbidden us to eat or even to touch, on pain of death. And the serpent said to her, What is this talk of death? God knows well that as soon as you eat this fruit your eyes will be opened, and you yourselves will be like gods, knowing good and evil. And with that the woman, who saw that the fruit was good to eat . . . took some . . . from the tree and ate it; and she gave some to her husband, and he ate with her. Then the eyes of both were opened, and they became aware of their nakedness; so they sewed fig-leaves together, and made themselves girdles.

And now they heard the voice of the Lord God, as he walked in the garden in the cool of the evening; whereupon Adam and his wife hid themselves in the garden, among the trees. And the Lord God called to Adam; Where art thou? he asked. I heard thy voice, Adam said, in the garden, and I was afraid, because of my nakedness, so I hid myself. And the answer came, Why, who told thee of thy nakedness? Or hadst thou eaten of the tree, whose fruit I forbade thee to eat? The woman, said Adam, whom thou gavest me to be my companion, she it was who offered me fruit from the tree, and so I came to eat it. Then the Lord God said to the woman, What made thee do this? The serpent, she said, beguiled me, and so I came to eat.

And the Lord God said to the serpent, For this work of thine, thou, alone among all the cattle and all the wild beasts, shall bear a curse; thou shalt crawl on thy belly and eat dust all thy life long. And I will establish a feud between thee and the woman, between thy offspring and hers; she is to crush thy head,△ whilst thou dost lie in wait at her heels. To the woman he said, Many are the pangs, many are the throes I will give thee to endure; with pangs thou shalt give birth to children, and thou shalt be subject to thy husband; he shall be thy lord. And to Adam he said, Thou hast listened to thy wife's counsel, and hast eaten the fruit I forbade thee to eat; and now, through thy act, the ground is under a curse. All the days of thy life thou shalt win food from it with toil; thorns and thistles it shall yield thee, this ground from which thou dost win thy food.

You can turn man back into dust by
saying, 'Back to what you were, you sons
of men!'
To you, a thousand years are a
single day, a yesterday now over, an
hour of the night.
You brush men away like waking
dreams, they are like grass
sprouting and flowering in the morning,
withered and dry before dusk.
(Psalm 90: iii—vi. Jerusalem Bible.)

ADAM AND EVE DRIVEN OUT OF PARADISE

So the Lord God drove him out from that garden of delight, to cultivate the ground from which he came; banished Adam, and posted his Cherubim before the garden of delight, with a sword of fire that turned this way and that, so that he could reach the tree of life no longer.

The principal things necessary for the
life of men, are water, fire, and iron,
salt, milk, and bread of flour,
and honey, and the cluster of the grape,
and oil, and clothing.
(Ecclesiasticus 39: xxxi. Douay.)

ADAM TILLING THE GROUND

The name which Adam gave his wife was Eve, Life, because she was the mother of all living men.

And now Adam had knowledge of his wife, Eve, and she conceived. She called her child Cain, as if she would say, Cana, I have been enriched by the Lord with a man-child. Then she bore a second time; this child, his brother, she called Abel. Abel became a shepherd, while Cain tilled the ground.

Man that is born of a woman
hath but a short time to live. . . .
He cometh up, and is cut down,
like a flower; he fleeth as it were a
shadow, and never continueth in one
stay.
(The Book of Common Prayer,
Burial Service.)

Time passed, and the race of men began to spread over the face of earth, they and the daughters that were born to them. . . .

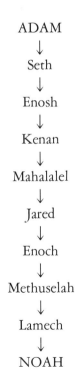

ADAM
↓
Seth
↓
Enosh
↓
Kenan
↓
Mahalalel
↓
Jared
↓
Enoch
↓
Methuselah
↓
Lamech
↓
NOAH

And now God found that earth was full of men's iniquities, and that the whole frame of their thought was set continually on evil; and he repented of having made men on the earth at all. So, smitten with indignation to the depths of his heart, he said, I will blot out mankind, my creature, from the face of the earth. . . . Only on Noah did God look with favour.

There lay the world, corrupt in God's sight, full of oppression; and God, seeing the world so corrupt (no creature on earth but had lost its true direction), said to Noah, The time has come for me to make an end of all mankind; their coming has filled the earth with oppression; I mean to destroy them, and earth with them. . . . Thou must know that I mean to bring a flood of waters over the earth, and destroy every creature that lives and breathes under heaven; all that earth holds must perish. But with thee this covenant of mine shall stand. . . .△

THE BUILDING OF THE ARK

Make thyself an ark from planks of wood; in that ark make cabins, and give it a coat of pitch within and without. These are to be the measurements; four hundred and fifty feet of length, seventy-five feet of breadth, and forty-five feet of height. The ark is to have a course of windows, which thou wilt make a foot and a half in height; and thou wilt make a door in its side; and it is to have a hold, and a lower and upper deck. . . .

All this Noah did, at God's bidding.

And now the Lord said to him, Take refuge in the Ark, with all thy household . . . thou and thy sons, and thy wife, and thy sons' wives with thee. And take with thee into the ark, to preserve them, a pair of each kind of living creature, male and female, all the different birds, all the different beasts, all the creeping things of earth; two of each shall go in with thee, so that all may survive. And it is for thee to provide thyself with all that is eaten as food, and store it up, so that thou and they may have food to eat. . . . In seven days from this, I mean to send down rain on the earth for forty days and forty nights, and blot out the whole world of living creatures from the face of the earth.

Keep me as the apple of the eye, hide me
under the shadow of thy wings, . . .
(Psalm 17: viii. Authorized Version.)

THE DELUGE

Seven days passed . . . and the flood-gates of heaven were opened. . . . That very day, Noah and his sons, Shem, Ham and Japheth, his wife, and the three wives of his sons, took refuge in the Ark; and with them all the different kinds of wild beasts, of cattle, of the creeping things of earth, and of things that fly, birds and winged creatures; there was refuge with Noah in the Ark for pairs of all mortal things that live and breathe. Into the Ark they went, males and females, as God had commanded; and the Lord shut him in.

For forty days that flood came down on the earth, and the water grew deep, till it lifted the Ark up from the ground; full the tide flowed, covering the whole face of the earth, but still the Ark rode safe on the waters. Higher and higher the waters rose above the ground, till all the high mountains under heaven disappeared; the flood stood fifteen cubits higher than the mountains it covered. All mortal things that moved on earth were drowned, birds and cattle and wild beasts, and all the creeping things of earth, and all mankind; all that lived and moved on the earth perished together. . . . Only Noah and his companions in the Ark were left. And the waters held their own over the land for a hundred and fifty days.

Then God bethought him of Noah, and of all the wild beasts and the cattle that went with him in the Ark; so he made his spirit pass over the earth, and with that, the waters abated. . . . And now, on the twenty-seventh day of the seventh month, the Ark came to rest upon the mountains of Ararat.△ Inch by inch the waters abated, until the tenth month came; on the first day of the tenth month, the hill tops began to shew. Noah let forty days pass, and then undid the opening he had made in the Ark, and sent out one of the ravens, which went this way and that, and had not come back to him when the waters dried up over the earth. Then . . . he sent out one of the doves. The dove could find no resting-place to perch on, so it came back to the Ark and its master; and he put out his hand to catch it, and took it back into the Ark. Seven days more he waited, and then sent the dove out from the Ark again; this time, it came back to him at night-fall, with a twig of olive in its mouth, the leaves still green on it; and then Noah made sure that the waters had become shallow all over the ground. . . . By the seventeenth day of the second month, the land itself was dry.

For, lo, the winter is past, the rain is
over and gone; the flowers appear on
the earth; the time of the singing of birds
is come, and the voice of the turtle
is heard in our land, . . .
(Song of Solomon 2: xi—xii.
Authorized Version.)

THE DESCENT FROM THE ARK

Then God's word came to Noah, telling him, Come out of the Ark, with thy wife and thy sons and their wives. Bring out with thee all the living creatures thou hast there . . . occupy this earth, increase and multiply upon it. So Noah came out, and his sons and his wife and his sons' wives with him; and the living creatures came out of the Ark. . . .

THE SACRIFICE OF NOAH

Thereupon Noah built an altar to the Lord, and chose out beasts that were clean and birds that were clean, and made burnt-offerings there. And the Lord, smelling such a scent as pleased him, made the resolve, Never again will I plague the earth on man's account . . . never again will I send affliction such as this upon all living creatures. While the earth stands, seed-time and harvest, cold and heat, summer and winter, day and night shall keep their course unaltered.

This, God said, shall be the pledge of the promise I am making to you . . . I will set my bow in the clouds, to be a pledge of my covenant with creation. When I veil the sky with clouds, in those clouds my bow shall appear. . . . There, in the clouds, my bow shall stand . . . covenant with all the life that beats in mortal creatures upon earth.

These were the descendants of Noah's son, Shem:

NOAH
↓
Shem
↓
Arphaxad
↓
Salah
↓
Eber
↓
Peleg
↓
Reu
↓
Serug
↓
Nahor
↓
Terah
↓
ABRAM

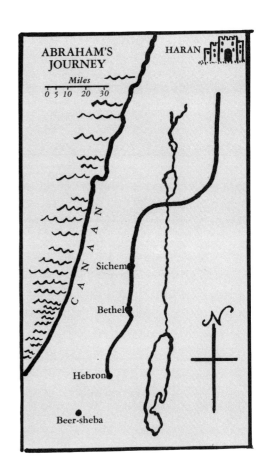

. . . the Lord said to Abram, Leave thy country behind thee, thy kinsfolk, and thy father's home, and come away into a land I will shew thee. Then I will make a great people of thee; I will bless thee, and make thy name renowned, a name of benediction; those who bless thee, I will bless, those who curse thee, I will curse, and in thee all the races of the world shall find a blessing. So Abram went out, as the Lord bade him, and with him went his nephew, Lot. Abram was seventy-five years old at the time when he left Haran,△ took his wife Sarai and his nephew Lot with him, all the possessions they had acquired in Haran, and all the retainers born in their service there, and set out for the land of Canaan. When they reached it, Abram went across country as far as Sichem and the Valley of Clear Seeing. Those were the days when the Canaanites still dwelt in the land. Here the Lord appeared to Abram, promising to give the whole land to his posterity; and this appearance he commemorated by building the Lord an altar there.

Thus Abram journeyed on, travelling always further south.

It chanced at this time that . . . the king of Sennaar, and . . . the king of Pontus, and . . . the king of Elam, and . . . the king of the barbarians, went out to war . . . and . . . the kings of Sodom and Gomorrha . . . came out to meet them. . . . The Valley of the Forests contains many pools of asphalt, and among these the kings of Sodom and Gomorrha were overcome and routed. . . . All the wealth of Sodom and Gomorrha, and all their supply of food, was carried off by the victors as they went; so, too, was Abram's nephew Lot. . . .

Abram himself, as soon as he heard that his brother△ Lot was a prisoner, mustered the men he had in arms . . . and went in pursuit.

He shone in his days as the morning
star in the midst of a cloud, and as the
moon at the full.
And as the sun when it shineth, so
did he shine in the temple of GOD.
(Ecclesiasticus 50: vi—vii. Douay.)

MELCHISEDECH AND ABRAHAM

He . . . fell upon the enemy by night, routing them and driving them in their flight as far as Hoba, to the left of Damascus; and he brought back all that wealth with him, Lot, too, and the wealth that was his, and the women, and the common folk.

And as he came back, the king of Sodom went out to meet him at the Valley of Savé, which is the same as the Royal Valley; Melchisedech, too, was there, the king of Salem. And he, priest as he was of the most high God, brought out bread and wine with him, and gave him this benediction, On Abram be the blessing of the most high God, maker of heaven and earth, and blessed be that most high God, whose protection has brought thy enemies into thy power. To him, Abram gave tithes of all he had won.

GOD'S PROMISE TO ABRAHAM

It was when Abram reached the age of ninety-nine that the Lord was revealed to him with the words, I am God Almighty; live as in my sight, and be perfect. Then, on my part, I will make a covenant with thee, to give thy posterity increase beyond measure. At this, Abram fell prostrate before him. And God said to him; I AM, and here is the covenant I make with thee, thou shalt be the father of a multitude of nations. No longer shall thy name be Abram, thou shalt be called Abraham, the father of a throng, such is the multitude of nations I will give thee for thy children.△ I will make thee fruitful beyond all measure, so that thou shalt count among the nations; from thy issue, kings shall arise. I will honour this covenant of mine with thyself and with the race that shall follow thee, generation after generation; an eternal covenant that pledges me to be thy God, and the God of the race which follows thee. To thee, and to that race, I will give the land in which thou dwellest now as a stranger, the whole land of Canaan; their inheritance for ever, and I their God.

This, too, God said to Abraham, Thou shalt call thy wife not Sarai△ but Sara, the princess. Her I will bless, giving thee a son by her; and him, too, I will bless, giving him whole nations for his posterity; kings with their peoples shall take their origin from him.

At this, Abraham fell prostrate before him; but in his heart he said, laughing at the thought, Shall I have a son when I am a hundred years old? Will Sara, with all her ninety years, become a mother?

ABRAHAM WITH THE THREE ANGELS

He had a vision of the Lord, too . . . as he sat by his tent door at noon. He looked up, and saw three men standing near him; and, at the sight, he ran from his tent door to meet them, bowing down to the earth. Lord, he said, as thou lovest me, do not pass thy servant by; let me fetch a drop of water, so that you can wash your feet and rest in the shade. I will bring a mouthful of food, too, so that you can refresh yourselves before you go on further. . . .

When they finished eating, they asked, Where is thy wife Sara? She is here, he answered, in the tent. I will come back, said he who was speaking to him, next year without fail; and, live she till then, thy wife Sara shall have a son. Sara, behind the tent door, overheard it and laughed. . . . What, she said, laughing to herself at the thought, am I to have dalliance with this lord of mine, grown old as I too have grown old? Whereupon the Lord said to Abraham, Why does Sara laugh . . . ? Can any task be too difficult for the Lord? . . . And when Sara, overcome with terror, denied the charge of laughing, Ah, he said, but thou didst laugh.

And now the men rose up, and turned towards Sodom, Abraham going with them to put them on their way. And the Lord said, Should I hide my purpose from Abraham, this man who is destined to give birth to a people so great and so powerful? . . . So the Lord told him, The ill repute of Sodom and Gomorrha goes from bad to worse, their sin is grievous out of all measure; I must needs go down to see for myself . . . I must know for certain.

Abraham drew close to him, and asked, Wilt thou, then, sweep away the innocent with the guilty? Suppose there are fifty innocent men in the city, must they too perish? . . . And the Lord told him, If I find fifty innocent citizens in Sodom, I will spare the whole place to save them. And Abraham answered . . . What if there should be five wanting to make up the tale of fifty innocent men? . . . No, he said, if I meet with forty-five such, I will not bring it to ruin. . . . And he said, Do not be angry with me, Lord, I entreat thee . . . what if ten are found there? I will spare it from destruction, he said, to save ten.

It was evening when the two angels reached Sodom, and Lot was sitting at the town gate. He rose up when he saw them, and went to meet them, bowing down his face to the earth. Pray, sirs, he said, turn in to my house and spend the night there. . . . So they went to his house, and he baked unleavened bread for them, which they ate. And before ever they had gone to rest, the townspeople laid siege to the house, old and young, from every quarter of the city, calling for Lot, and crying out, Where are thy evening visitors? Bring them out here, to minister to our lust. So Lot went out, shutting the door behind him, and said, No, brethren, I entreat you, do not be guilty of such a wrong. I have two daughters here, that have as yet no knowledge of man; these I will bring out, and you shall have your will with them, but do these men no harm; are they not guests under my roof? What, said they, wouldst thou . . . set thyself up as a judge? Stand back, or it will be worse for thee than for them. And they pushed Lot aside with great violence, trying to break the door in. So the two men [angels] reached out and pulled Lot back into the house, shutting the door after him; and they put a ban of blindness on the folk without, so that never a man of them could find the entry.

Then morning came, and the angels were urgent with Lot; Up, they said, take thy wife with thee, and the two daughters who are still at home, or else thou too wilt perish with the offending city. And when they found that he hung back, they pulled him away, with his wife and his two daughters, so resolved was the Lord to spare him; led him out, and set him clear of the city. Here they said to him, Flee for thy life, never once looking behind thee, never lingering once in all the plain round about thee; take refuge in the hills, or thou, too, wilt perish.

Where there is no vision, the people
perish: . . .
(Proverbs 29: xviii. Authorized Version.)

THE BURNING OF SODOM

. . . thereupon the Lord rained down brimstone and fire out of heaven, the Lord's dwelling-place, and overthrew these cities, with all the plain about them, and all those who dwelt there, and all that grew from their soil. And Lot's wife, because she looked behind her as she went, was turned into a pillar of salt.△

And now, true to his undertaking, the Lord visited Sara and fulfilled his promise; old as she was, she conceived and bore a son at the very time God had foretold. To this son whom Sara had borne him, Abraham gave the name of Isaac, and circumcised him, as God had commanded, when he was eight days old. He himself was then a hundred years old; so great an age had he reached before Isaac was born to him. And Sara cried out, God has made me laugh for joy; whoever hears of this will laugh (Isaac) with me.

After this, God would put Abraham to the test. So he called to him, Abraham, Abraham; and when he said, I am here, at thy command, God told him, Take thy only son, thy beloved son Isaac, with thee, to the land of Clear Vision, and there offer him to me in burnt sacrifice on a mountain which I will shew thee. Rising, therefore, at dawn, Abraham saddled his ass, bidding two of the men-servants and his son Isaac follow him; he cut the wood needed for the burnt sacrifice, and then set out for the place of which God had spoken to him. It was two days later when he looked up and saw it, still far off; and now he said to his servants, Wait here with the ass, while I and my son make our way yonder; we will come back to you, when we have offered worship there. Then he took the wood for the sacrifice, and gave it to his son Isaac to carry; he himself carried the brazier and the knife. As they walked along together, Isaac said to him, Father. What is it, my son? he asked. Why, said he, we have the fire here and the wood; where is the victim we are to sacrifice? My son, said Abraham, God will see to it that he has a victim. So they went on together till they reached the place God had shewn him. And here he built an altar, and set the wood in order on it; then he bound his son Isaac and laid him down there on the altar, above the pile of wood. And he reached out, and took up the knife, to slay his son. But now, from heaven, an angel of the Lord called to him, Abraham, Abraham. And when he answered, Here am I, at thy command, the angel said, Do the lad no hurt, let him alone. I know now that thou fearest God; for my sake thou wast ready to give up thy only son. And Abraham looking about him, saw behind him a ram caught by the horns in a thicket; this he took and offered it as a burnt sacrifice, instead of his son. So Abraham called that spot, The Lord will see to it; and the saying goes to this day, On the mountain top, the Lord will see to it.

Abraham left Isaac the heir to all he possessed and made gifts to the children he had by his concubines. These children of his he bade journey eastwards, while he was still alive, to keep them apart from his son Isaac. Abraham lived a hundred and seventy-five years; then his strength failed him, and he died, content in late old age, his tale of years complete, and he became a part of his people.△ . . . And now that he was dead, God's blessing passed to his son Isaac, who had made his home close to the well that is called, God lives and looks on me.

. . . they that be wise shall shine as
the brightness of the firmament; and they
that turn many to righteousness as
the stars for ever and ever.
(Daniel 12: iii. Authorized Version.)

GOD COMMANDS ISAAC△

. . . a famine came upon the land . . . Isaac was for leaving it; and he had reached the court of Abimelech, king of the Philistines, in Gerara, when the Lord appeared to him, and said, No, do not take refuge in Egypt; thou art to remain in the land of my choice. Dwell in that land, though it be alien soil, and I will be with thee and bless thee; I mean to give all this land to thee and to thy race after thee, in fulfilment of the oath I took to thy father Abraham. I will make that race plentiful as the stars in heaven. . . .

And this was how the race of Abraham's son Isaac continued; Abraham was the father of Isaac, and Isaac was forty years old when he married Laban's sister Rebecca. . . .

ISAAC, REBECCA, AND ABIMELECH

And now, when certain of the inhabitants asked him about his wife Rebecca, he told them, She is my sister; he was afraid to own that she was his wedded wife, thinking they might be tempted by her beauty to kill him. And one day, when he had already spent a long time in the country, the . . . king, Abimelech, looked out of a window and saw Isaac and his wife in dalliance together. Whereupon he summoned him, and said, It is plain enough, now, that she is thy wife, why didst thou pretend she was thy sister? I was afraid, Isaac answered, that she might be the cause of my death. What is this trick thou hast played on us? said Abimelech. One of my people might easily have dishonoured thy wife, and so thou wouldst have led us into grievous guilt.

. . . At first Rebecca was barren, but Isaac prayed to the Lord for her, and his prayer was answered; Rebecca conceived. But the children fell to struggling in her womb; How am I the better for conceiving, she asked, if this is to befall me? And she went to ask counsel from the Lord. The answer he gave was this: There are two nations in thy womb; in thy body the separation of two peoples has begun. . . .

The time came for her giving birth, and it was found that there had been twins in her womb. The first to come was of a red complexion, and hairy all over as if he had worn a coat of skin; this one was called Esau. Then the second came, with his hand clutching his brother's heel; and she called him, for that reason, Jacob, the Supplanter.

And now Isaac was old, and his eyes had grown so dim that he saw nothing. One day he called to his elder son Esau, My son! and when he answered, I am here, at thy command, See, his father said, how old a man I have grown; there is no telling how soon I may be overtaken by death. Come, fetch that armoury of thine, thy quiver and thy bow, and go out hunting; when thou has slain thy quarry, make me a roast dish, such as I love well, and bring it me to eat. And so thou shalt have my blessing, against the time of my death.

To all this, Rebecca listened; and when Esau had gone out hunting, to do as his father had bidden him, she said to her son Jacob . . . Make thy way to the herd, and bring me two choice kids; of these I will make such a dish as thy father loves to eat, and thou shalt take it in to him; so . . . his dying benediction shall be thine. . . . So Jacob went and brought them to his mother, and she made a dish of meat. . . . She had fine clothes of Esau's by her in the house, and she dressed Jacob in these; enclosed his hands, too, in skin he had taken from the kids, and covered his bare neck with it; then she gave him the dish, and some loaves which she had cooked, to carry with him.

The first wrote, Wine is the strongest.
The second wrote, The king is strongest.
The third wrote, Women are strongest.
(I Esdras 3: x—xii. Authorized Version.)

ISAAC BLESSES JACOB

So Jacob brought them in, and said, Father. Yes, my son, he said; who is it? I am Esau, said Jacob, Esau, thy first-born; I have done thy bidding. Rise up, I pray thee, sit at table, and eat this venison of mine, and give me a father's blessing. . . . Then Isaac said, Come near, and let me feel thee, to make sure whether thou art my son Esau or not. So he went close to his father; and he, upon feeling the touch of him, said, The voice is Jacob's voice, but the hands are the hands of Esau. . . . Thou art my son, he said, my son Esau? Yes, he answered, I am. Why then, said he, bring it here; let me eat my son's venison, and give him a father's blessing. . . .

Then he said to Jacob, Come here, my son, and kiss me. And when he came near, and kissed him, all at once Isaac caught the smell of his garments, and this was the blessing he gave him: How it breathes about this son of mine, the fragrance of earth when the Lord's blessing is on it! God give thee dew from heaven and fruitful soil, corn and wine in plenty. Let nations serve thee, and peoples bow before thee; mayest thou be lord over thy brethren, receive obeisance from thy own mother's sons; a curse on those who curse, a blessing on those who bless thee!

Scarcely had Isaac finished speaking, and Jacob gone out, when Esau returned. And now he brought his father a dish of venison; Rise up, father, he said, eat thy son's venison, and give me a father's blessing. Why, who art thou? Isaac asked. I am thy son, he answered, thy first-born son Esau. At this, quite overcome with dread, astonished past belief, Isaac cried out, Why then, who is it that has already brought me venison . . . ? I have eaten my fill, and . . . on him the blessing will come.

ESAU BEGS FOR A BLESSING

Esau, on hearing his father's words, broke out into a loud cry of anguish; Thy blessing, father, for me also thy blessing! Thy brother, it seems, Isaac answered, came in disguised; he has snatched thy blessing from thee. Why, said Esau, he is well named Jacob, the Supplanter. . . . Hast thou no blessing left, then, a blessing for me too? Nay, answered Isaac, I have designated him thy master; I have condemned all his brethren to do him service; I have assured him of corn and wine; what claim have I left myself to make for thee, my son? But Esau pleaded still, Hast thou only one blessing to give, father? . . . Then Isaac said, greatly moved, All thy blessing shall come from earth's fruitfulness, and from the dew of heaven. . . . Thou shalt be subject to thy brother, until the day comes when thou wilt rebel, and wilt shake off his yoke from thy neck.

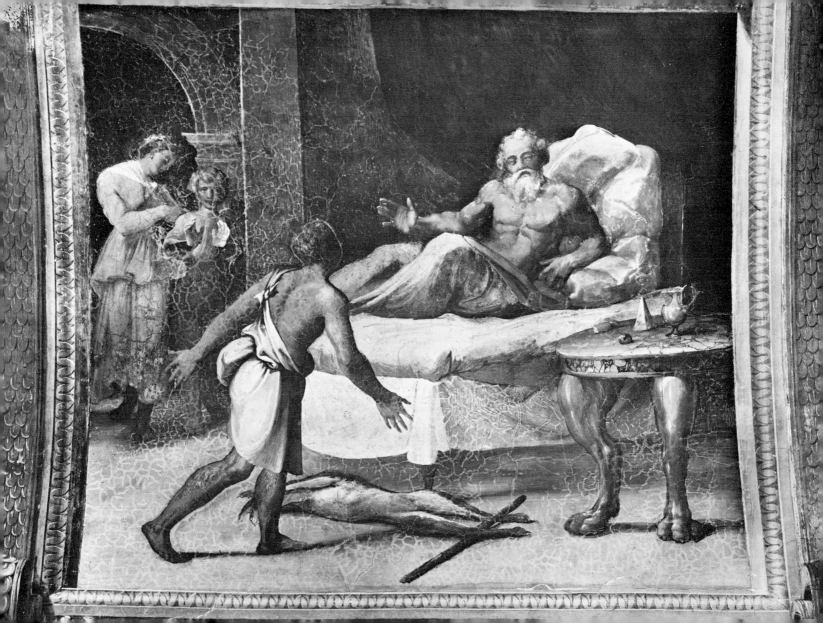

. . . Isaac summoned Jacob to him, and gave him his blessing, and laid this charge upon him: It is not for thee to marry a woman of Canaanite stock; rather bestir thyself, and make thy way to Mesopotamia of the Syrians . . . there thou mayest wed one of the daughters of thy uncle Laban. . . .

Jacob took leave of him, and set out on his journey. . . .

For he hath given his angels charge over thee; to keep thee in all thy ways. (Psalm 90: xi. Douay.)

JACOB'S DREAM△

There was a place he reached as nightfall overtook him, so that he must lie down and rest; so he took some of the stones that lay around him, to make a pillow of them, and went to sleep. He dreamed that he saw a ladder standing on the earth, with its top reaching up into heaven; a stairway for the angels of God to go up and come down. Over this ladder the Lord himself leaned down, and spoke to Jacob, I am the Lord, he said, the God of thy father Abraham, the God of Isaac; this ground on which thou liest sleeping is my gift to thee and to thy posterity. Thy race shall be countless as the dust of the earth; to west and east, to north and south thou shalt overflow thy frontiers, till all the families on earth find a blessing in thee, and in this race of thine. I myself will watch over thee wherever thou goest, and bring thee back to this land again; before I have done with thee, all my promises to thee shall be fulfilled. . . .

Then Jacob went on his way, and reached the eastern country.

Behold, thou art fair, my love; behold,
thou art fair; Thine eyes are as doves.
(Song of Songs 1: xv. Revised Version.)

JACOB AT THE WELL

Here, in the open plain, he found a well, with three flocks of sheep lying down beside it. It was here that the flocks were watered; but the mouth of the well was closed by a great stone, and it was not the custom to roll this stone away till all the flocks were assembled. . . . Whence come you, brethren? he asked the shepherds. From Haran, they answered. And his next question was, whether they knew Laban. . . . Yes, they said, we know him. . . . That is his daughter, Rachel, yonder, coming towards us with her flock. . . .

Jacob watched her as she came. . . .

As cold water to a thirsty soul, so is good tidings from a far country. (Proverbs 25: xxv. Douay.)

LABAN MEETS JACOB

This was Jacob's cousin, these were his uncle Laban's sheep; so he moved away the stone by which the well was shut in. Then, when she had watered her flock, he went up and kissed her, weeping aloud; and he told her that he was her father's kinsman, Rebecca's son; whereupon she went quickly home to tell her father the news.

No sooner did Laban hear of his nephew Jacob's arrival, than he ran out to meet him, embraced him, covered him with kisses, and brought him back home.

Laban had two daughters; Rachel was the younger and her elder sister was called Leah. But Leah was dull-eyed, whereas Rachael had beauty both of form and face, and on her Jacob's love had fallen. . . .

So Jacob worked seven years to win Rachel, and they seemed to him only a few days, because of the greatness of his love.

Then he said to Laban, Give me my bride; the time has come now for me to wed her. So Laban invited a great company of his friends to the wedding feast; but that night he matched Jacob with his daughter Leah instead. . . . With all due ceremony, Jacob took her to his bed, and it was not till morning he found out that it was Leah. Whereupon he said to Laban, What meanest thou? Did not I work for thee to win Rachel? What is this trick thou hast played on me? And Laban answered, It is not the custom of our country to wed our younger daughters first. Celebrate this wedding of thine for a full week, and I will give thee Rachel too, and thou shalt work for me another seven years to earn her. . . . So, at last, Jacob won the bride he had longed for, and loved her better than he had loved her sister. . . .

And now, seeing Leah thus despised, the Lord gave her issue, while Rachel must remain barren.

Rachel, meanwhile, when she found she remained barren, looked with envy on her sister; Thou must needs give me children, said she to her husband, or it will be my death. What, answered Jacob, angry at her mood, Must I stand in the place of God to thee? It is he that has denied thee motherhood. Here is Bilbah, she said, my maid-servant; get her with child instead, and it shall be born on my knees; thus, through her means, I shall have a family of my own. . . . Bilbah, got with child by Rachel's husband, bore a son.

Meanwhile, the Lord had not forgotten Rachel; her prayer was answered, and she, too, had issue. When she conceived and bore a son, her thought was, God has taken away my disgrace. And she called him Joseph, Increase. . . .

Laban's sons were complaining, Our father has been robbed of all his goods by Jacob, who has become rich at his expense. Jacob was aware of this. . . . But what moved him most was that the Lord had bidden him, Return to the land of thy fathers, to thy own kindred.

He mounted his children and wives on camels,△ and set out on his journey; taking with him all his possessions, his cattle and all the wealth he had gained; he would return to his father Isaac, and the land of Canaan.

Jacob had given his father-in-law no warning of his flight, and it was not till he and all that belonged to him had gone away, and crossed the Euphrates, and were making for the hills of Gilead, that a message came to Laban, three days too late, Jacob has fled. So now Laban took his kinsmen with him and gave chase; and . . . overtook him on the hills of Gilead. . . . What meanest thou, he asked Jacob, by thus tricking me, and carrying off my daughters as if they were prisoners of war? Why wouldst thou run away when my back was turned, instead of warning me of it, so that I could have sped thee on thy way with good cheer, with singing, and music of timbrel and harp? . . .

To this Jacob answered, If I left thee unawares, it was because I was afraid thou wouldst rob me of thy daughters by violence. . . . And Laban answered, These are my daughters, these boys are mine, as thy flocks, and all thou seest before thee, are mine; something I must do to protect my own daughters, my own grandchildren. Come, let us make a covenant, which shall stand on record between us.

So Jacob took a stone, and set it up there as a monument. . . .

'. . . wherever you go, I will go, wherever
you live, I will live.
Your people shall be my people, and your
God, my God.
Wherever you die, I will die. . . .'
(Ruth 1: xvi—xvii. Jerusalem Bible.)

PARTING OF JACOB WITH LABAN

. . . Laban rose up at daybreak, kissed his grandsons and his two daughters, and blessed them, and went back to his home.

Jacob, too, set out to continue his journey. . . .

And now he sent messengers of his own on before him, to greet his brother Esau in the country of Seir. . . .

And this was the news the messengers brought back with them, We found thy brother Esau; even now he comes hastening to meet thee, with four hundred men. At this, Jacob was overcome with terror . . . and said, O God of my father Abraham . . . Save me now from the power of my brother Esau. . . .

He chose out of all his possessions a present for his brother Esau, two hundred she-goats and twenty buck-goats, two hundred ewes and twenty rams, thirty camels in milk with their colts, forty cows and twenty bulls, and twenty she-asses with ten colts. All these he sent on, with their drivers . . . and he waited in the camp all night.

And now Jacob looked in front of him, and there was Esau coming towards him, with four hundred men at his back. So he divided up his children into families, Leah's sons and Rachel's and those of the two serving-women. He put these first with their children, and Leah second with hers; Rachel and Joseph came last of all. He himself, as he came up, prostrated himself seven times before his brother reached him. Seeing this, Esau ran to meet his brother, embraced him, clung to his neck, and kissed him, in tears. . . . Then he said, Let us travel on together. . . . But Jacob answered . . . Pass on, my lord, in advance of thy servant; I will follow slowly, at whatever pace suits these children of mine, and meet thee again, my lord, in Seir. . . .

So that day, Esau went back to Seir. . . . Jacob went as far as Socoth, and there built himself a house. . . . He passed on from there to Salem . . . thus returning to Canaan. . . . Here he dwelt near the town; he bought the piece of ground where he encamped . . . at the price of a hundred lambs.

. . . Joseph was sixteen years old, and helped his brethren to feed their flocks, young though he was. . . . Among his children, Jacob loved Joseph best, as old men love the sons old age has brought them; and he dressed him in a coat that was all embroidery.^Δ Whereupon his brethren, who saw that he was his father's favourite, bore him a grudge, and never had a good word for him.

JOSEPH TELLS HIS DREAM△

They hated him the more, when Joseph recounted to them a dream of his; Listen, he said, to this dream I have had. I dreamt that we were all binding sheaves in a field, and my sheaf seemed to lift itself up and stand erect, while all your sheaves stood about it and did reverence to mine. What, said his brethren, art thou to be our king? Are we to be thy subjects? . . . Then he had another dream which he disclosed to his brethren; In this dream of mine, he said, it seemed to me that the sun and the moon and eleven stars did reverence to me. When he reported this to his father and his brethren, his father said, in reproof, What means this dream of thine? Must I and thy mother and thy brethren bow down to earth before thee?

One day, when his brethren were away at Sichem, feeding their flocks, Israel [Jacob] said to Joseph, Thy brethren are pasturing their sheep at Sichem; I have an errand for thee there. And when Joseph answered, I am here, at thy command, he said to him, Go and see whether all is well with thy brethren, and with the flock, then come back and tell me their news. . . . So Joseph went on in search of his brethren, and it was at Dothain he found them. Before he came up to them, they caught sight of him in the distance, and began plotting against his life. They said to one another, Here comes the dreamer; how if we kill him, and throw his body into a dry well? We can pretend he has fallen a prey to some wild beast. Now we shall see what good these dreams of his can do him! Upon this, Reuben began scheming to save Joseph from their violence; No, he said, do not take his life, there must be no bloodshed. Throw him down into this well here, far from all help, and so keep clear of any murderous act. His meaning was to rescue Joseph out of their hands, and restore him safe to his father. As soon, then, as Joseph reached his brethren, they stripped him of his long, embroidered coat, and threw him into a disused well, which had no water left in it.

JOSEPH TAKEN OUT OF THE WELL

And now, as they sat down to take their meal, they saw a company of Ishmaelites mounted on camels, who were on their way from Gilead to Egypt, with a load of spices, balm, and myrrh. Whereupon Judah said to his brethren, What shall we gain by killing our brother, and concealing his murder? Far better sell him to these Ishmaelites, and keep our hands clean of crime; remember that he is our brother, our own flesh and blood. His brethren fell in with the plan; so, when the merchants . . . passed by, they dragged Joseph up out of the well, and sold him for twenty pieces of silver to these Ishmaelites, who carried him off with them to Egypt.

. . . Joseph's brethren killed a goat, and dipped Joseph's coat in its blood; then they sent a message to their father, We have found this coat; satisfy thyself whether it is thy son's, or not. And their father recognized it . . . past doubt, some wild thing has devoured him, my son Joseph, the prey of a wild beast! And he tore his garments, and put on sackcloth; and long he mourned for his son. Vainly did all his children conspire to solace their father's grief; he would admit no consolation.

Meanwhile, Joseph had been taken away into Egypt, where his Ishmaelite owners sold him to an Egyptian called Potiphar, one of Pharaoh's courtiers, and captain of his guard. The Lord was with him, so that he prospered in all he undertook; and he was given a lodging in the house of his master. . . . Thus Joseph became his master's favourite servant, and had the management of all his affairs, and of all the property that was entrusted to him. . . .

Joseph had beauty of form and face, and after a while his mistress cast longing eyes at him, and bade him share her bed. But he would have nothing to do with such wickedness; My master, he said, entrusts everything to my care, and keeps no count of his belongings; there is nothing of his but I, by his appointment, have the keeping of it, save thee only, his wedded wife. How canst thou ask me to wrong him so grievously, and offend my God? Such was the talk between them day after day, she ever more importunate, and he still resisting her shameful desire.

A golden ring in the snout of a pig is a
lovely woman who lacks discretion.
(Proverbs 2: xxii. Jerusalem Bible.)

JOSEPH AND POTIPHAR'S WIFE

A day came at last when Joseph must needs be within doors, busy with some task when no one else was by; and she caught him by the hem of his garment, inviting him to her bed. Whereupon he went out, leaving his cloak still in her hand.

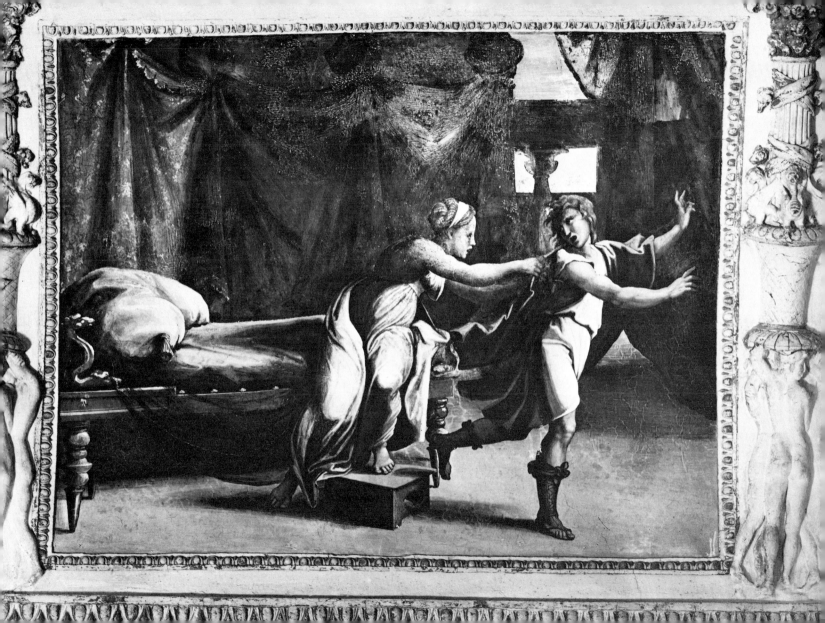

And now, finding herself alone with his garment in her hands, and all her advances spurned, she summoned the men of the household; Look, she said, what comes of bringing in a Hebrew to insult us! Joseph came in, and would have dishonoured me, but I cried out, and at the sound of my voice he ran out, leaving his cloak in my grasp. She kept the cloak in support of her story, and shewed it to her husband when he came back home. . . . Upon this Joseph's master, too easily convinced by what his wife told him, broke into a rage, and committed Joseph to the prison in which the king's prisoners were kept. There lay Joseph, then, a captive, but the Lord was still with him, and by the Lord's mercy he became a favourite with the chief gaoler, who put all the prisoners detained there in his charge, and would have nothing done save at his discretion.

Then, two years afterwards, Pharaoh . . . had a dream. He thought that he was standing by the Nile, and out of its channel there came up seven heifers, sleek and well fattened, which began feeding on the river bank, among the reeds. Then seven others

came up, also out of the river, ill-favoured and ill-nourished; and these too stood graz-
ing where it was green, close to the river. And it seemed as if they ate up those other
seven, that were so fine and well fed. With that Pharaoh awoke, and when he slept
again, it was to dream a second dream. This time, there were seven ears of corn growing
from a single stalk, all plump and fair, and another seven ears, all shrunken and
blighted, came up in their turn, to eat up the fair promise of the other seven. Pharaoh,
then, awoke from his dream, and as soon as it was daylight, he sent for all the diviners
and all the wise men of Egypt. When they answered his summons, he told them of his
dream, without finding anyone who could interpret it.

And now, at last, the chief cup-bearer remembered. . . . When thou, my lord, wast
vexed with thy servants, thou didst commit me and thy chief cook to prison, with the
captain of thy guard in charge of us; and there, on a single night . . . we had a dream
which foretold what was to become of us. One of our fellow-prisoners, a Hebrew slave,
belonging to this same captain, heard what our dreams were, and gave us an account
of them which the event proved right. . . .

. . . your old men shall dream dreams,
and your young men shall see visions.
(Joel 2: xxviii. Douay.)

JOSEPH EXPLAINS PHARAOH'S DREAM

With that, the king sent to have Joseph released from prison and brought before him, with his beard shaved and new clothes to wear. I have had certain dreams, he said, and no one can tell me the meaning of them; I have heard of thee as one who can interpret such things with sovereign skill. No skill of mine is needed, said Joseph; the Lord will give Pharaoh his answer, and a favourable one.

So Pharaoh described what he had seen. . . . My lord, answered Joseph, the two dreams are all one, God is warning my lord Pharaoh of what he intends to do. The seven sleek cattle, the seven plump ears, have the same sense in the two dreams; they stand for seven years of plenty. Whereas the seven gaunt, starved cattle which came up after them, and the seven shrunken, blighted ears of corn, prophesy seven years of famine. . . .

It is for thee, my lord king, to find some man that has the wisdom and the skill for it, and put the whole of Egypt under his charge. He must appoint a commissioner for each region, to collect a fifth of the harvest during the seven years of plenty which are now upon us, and store it up in barns. . . . If not, the whole land will perish for want of it.

The plan commended itself to Pharaoh and to all his courtiers. And now he asked them, Where are we to find another man such as this, so full of God's inspiration? Then he turned to Joseph, and said, Every word thou hast spoken comes to thee revealed by God, and shall I look for some other whose wisdom can match thine? Thou shalt have charge of my household, and all my people shall obey thy word of command; thou shalt share all I have, except this royal throne. Hereby, Pharaoh said to Joseph, I put the whole land of Egypt under thy care. . . .

So Joseph set out on his mission to the land of Egypt, having thus won the favour of king Pharaoh when he was only thirty years old; and there was no part of Egypt he did not visit. Seven years of abundance came, and the corn was bound in sheaves and taken away to all the storehouses that could be found in Egypt. . . .

So the first seven years passed, years of plenty for Egypt; and now, as Joseph had prophesied, seven years of scarcity began; famine reigned all over the world, but everywhere in Egypt there was bread to be had. . . . Soon the whole world was coming to Egypt and buying food to relieve its want.

The news that there was corn to be bought in Egypt reached Jacob among the rest; and he said to his sons, What means this lethargy? . . . Why do you not go down there, and buy enough for us to live on, instead of waiting till we starve? So ten of Joseph's brethren went down into Egypt to buy corn there; only Benjamin his father kept at home, saying to the others, Some harm might befall him on the way. . . .

Egypt was under the control of Joseph; it was at his discretion that corn was sold to foreign nations. And when his brethren came and did him reverence, he recognized them; but he treated them as strangers, and talked roughly to them. Whence come you? he asked. . . . You are spies, he told them; you have come to find out where our country's defences are weak. No, my lord, they said, we are thy servants, come here to buy food, sons of one father, all of us, sent on an errand of peace. . . . Our father, in the land of Canaan, is the father of twelve sons; the youngest is still with him, and one of us no longer lives. I was sure of it, said he; you are spies, all of you. I will put you to the test; your youngest brother must come here, or, by the life of Pharaoh, none of you shall leave this land. . . . To prove whether your errand is peaceful, one of you must be kept here in prison; the rest shall go home. . . . Then you must bring your youngest brother here into my presence. . . .

When they came back to their father Jacob, in Canaan, they told him of all that had happened. . . . No, said he, I will not let this son of mine go with you. . . .

But still the land was famine-stricken, and all the food they had brought with them from Egypt was used up. . . . And their father Israel said to them . . . go back to the man, taking your brother with you. . . .

They took Benjamin down into Egypt, and presented themselves before Joseph. . . . Then Joseph looked . . . and saw Benjamin there, his own mother's son. . . .

Joseph could contain himself no longer, and there were many standing by. So he gave orders that all these should leave his presence; there must be no strangers to see it, when he made himself known. But when he spoke, he burst into such a fit of weeping that these Egyptians, and all Pharaoh's household, could not but hear it. I am Joseph, said he to his brethren; is my father yet alive? But his brethren were too much dismayed to answer him, and he must needs use gentleness. . . .

Make haste, go back to my father, and give him this message from his son Joseph: God has made me ruler of all Egypt; make thy way here with all speed. Thou shalt have the land of Gessen for thy dwelling-place, so that thou canst live close to me, with thy children and thy grandchildren, thy sheep and cattle and all that is thine. . . .

The sons of Israel did as they were bidden. . . . They left Egypt, and when they reached their father Jacob in Canaan, they gave him their news, Thy son Joseph is still alive, and it is he that rules the whole land of Egypt. Jacob heard it, with the look of one just awoken from a heavy sleep. . . . If my son Joseph, he said, is still alive, that is all I ask; I will go with you, and have sight of him again before I die.

Thus Jacob went into Egypt with sixty-six companions all sprung from his stock, not reckoning his sons' wives. Meanwhile, Joseph had had two sons born to him in Egypt, so that Jacob's whole clan, when they found a home in Egypt, reached the number of seventy.

Thus Israel began to find a home in Egypt . . . settled down there, and flourished, and grew great.

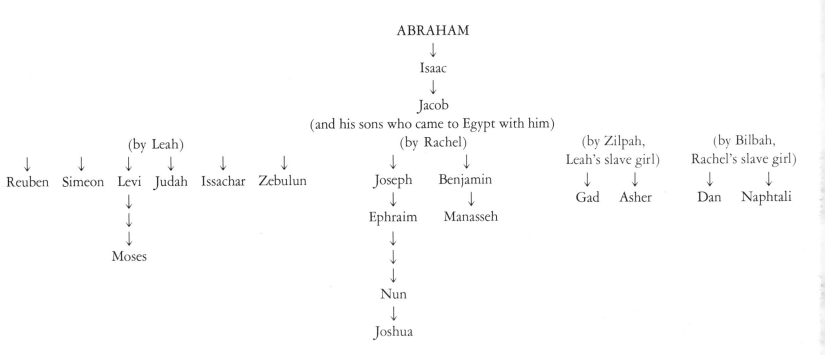

... the race of Israel [in Egypt] grew into a teeming multitude. ... Meanwhile, a new king had arisen, who knew nothing of Joseph. See, he said to his people, how the race of Israelites has grown. ... We must ... keep them down. ... So he appointed officers ... who laid crushing burdens on them. ... The Egyptians, in their abhorrence for the Israelites, oppressed and insulted them, making their lives a burden with drudgery in the clay-pit and the brick-kiln, drudgery, too, of all kinds in the cultivation of the land.

Then the king of Egypt gave orders to . . . the midwives who attended the Hebrews;
When you are called in, he said, to attend the Hebrew women, and their time comes,
kill the child if it is a boy; if it is a girl keep it alive. But these midwives feared the
Lord, and would not carry out the commands of the king of Egypt; they kept the boys
safe. . . . And at last Pharaoh made a proclamation to the whole of his people: Whenever a male child is born, cast it into the river. . . .

And now one of the descendants of Levi wooed and married a woman of his own clan, who conceived and bore him a son. So winning were the child's looks, that for three months she kept him hidden away; then, unable to conceal him any longer, she took a little basket of reeds, which she smeared with clay and pitch, and in this put her baby son down among the bulrushes on the river bank. The boy's sister waited at a distance, to see what would happen.

He shall be as a tree that is planted
by running waters, that yieldeth its fruit
in due season.
And whose leaves shall not wither: and
whatsoever he doeth shall prosper.
(Psalm 1: iii–iv. Monastic Diurnal,
St. Joseph, Minnesota.)

MOSES BROUGHT FROM THE WATER△

Just then, Pharaoh's daughter came down to bathe in the river, while her maid-servants walked along the bank. She caught sight of the basket among the rushes, and sent one of her attendants to fetch it; and when she opened it, and saw the baby crying, her heart was touched. Why, she said, this must be one of the Hebrew children. And at that, the boy's sister asked, Wouldst thou have me go and fetch one of the Hebrew women, to nurse the child for thee? Go by all means, she said; and the girl went and fetched her mother. Take this boy, Pharaoh's daughter said, and nurse him for me; I will reward thee for it. So the woman took the boy and nursed him till he was grown; then she handed him over to Pharaoh's daughter, who adopted him as her own son, and gave him the name of Moses, the Rescuer; I had to rescue him, she said, from the river.

A time came when Moses, now a grown-up man, went out among his brethren the Hebrews, and saw how ill they were treated, saw one of these brethren of his being beaten by an Egyptian; whereupon, after looking this way and that to see that no one was near, he killed the Egyptian and buried him there in the sand. . . . When Pharaoh heard of it, he was for putting Moses to death; and Moses, to avoid his scrutiny, took refuge in the country of Midian.

Then, after a long while, the king of Egypt died, and the cry of the Israelites, still groaning aloud in their drudgery, went up to God, who took pity on this drudgery of theirs, and listened to their complaint; he had not forgotten the covenant which he made with Abraham, Isaac, and Jacob.

MOSES AND THE BURNING BUSH

Moses, in the meanwhile, had married the daughter of Jethro, priest of Midian, and was doing shepherd's work for him. Deep into the desert he led his flock, till he reached God's own mountain of Horeb. And here the Lord revealed himself through a flame that rose up from the midst of a bush; it seemed that the bush was alight, yet did not burn. Here is a great sight, said Moses, I must go up and see more of it, a bush that does not waste by burning. But now, as he saw him coming up to look closer, the Lord called to him from the midst of the bush, Moses, Moses; and when he answered, I am here, at thy command, he was told, Do not come nearer; rather take the shoes from thy feet, thou art standing on holy ground.

Then he said, I am the God thy father worshipped, the God of Abraham, and Isaac, and Jacob. And Moses hid his face; he dared not look on the open sight of God.

I have not been blind, the Lord told him, to the oppression which my people endures in Egypt. . . . I know what their sufferings are, and I have come down to rescue them from the power of the Egyptians; to take them away into a fruitful land and large, a land that is all milk and honey. . . . Up, I have an errand for thee at Pharaoh's court; thou art to lead my people, the sons of Israel, away out of Egypt.

At this, Moses said to God, Ah, who am I, that thou shouldst send me to Pharaoh? . . . I will be with thee, God said to him.

But Moses still had his answer; What if they will not believe me, he said, or give a hearing? . . . What is that in thy hand? the Lord asked him. A staff, he said. So the Lord bade him cast it on the ground, and when he did so, it turned into a serpent, and Moses shrank away. Now put out thy hand, the Lord said, and catch it by the tail. He did so, and it turned to a staff in his hand.

Then Moses said, Lord, have patience with me . . . all my life I have been a man of little eloquence, and now that thou, my Master, hast spoken to me, I am more faltering, more tongue-tied than ever. Why, the Lord said to him, who was it that fashioned man's mouth? . . . Go as thou art bidden. . . . But still he said, Lord, have patience with me; wilt thou not choose some fitting emissary? And now the Lord was angry with Moses; What of thy brother Aaron (the Levite)? he asked. . . . He shall be thy spokesman. . . .

Then Moses made his way back to his father-in-law, Jethro; Give me leave, he said, to return to Egypt, and see whether my brethren there are still living. And Jethro said, Go in peace.

After this, Moses and Aaron obtained audience with Pharaoh, and said to him, We have a message to thee from the Lord God of Israel, Give my people leave to go and offer me sacrifice in the desert. Why, he answered, who is this Lord, that I must obey his command . . . ? I know no such Lord as that; I will not let Israel go.

And the Lord said to Moses . . . Then Egypt shall feel the weight of my hand. . . . Many signs, many portents will I give in this land of Egypt. . . .△

the rivers turned to blood
the frogs came up till the whole land of Egypt was full of them
the whole land stank with them
all over Egypt the dust on the ground turned to gnats
a grievous swarm of flies tainted the whole land everywhere:
the beasts belonging to the Egyptians died
ulcers and boils broke out on man and beast
thunder and hail and fire ran along the ground
locusts covered the whole face of the ground:
all over the land of Egypt utter darkness fell

But still . . . Pharaoh . . . would not let the Israelites go.

The Lord . . . told Moses, I mean to send one more plague on Pharaoh, and Egypt with him; after that he will let you go, nay, he will drive you out with all eagerness. . . .

At midnight I will make my way through the midst of Egypt, and with that every first-born thing in the land of Egypt will die, whether it be the first-born of Pharaoh, where he sits on his throne, or the first-born of the slave-woman working at the mill; all the first-born, too, of . . . cattle. All over the land of Egypt there shall be loud lament, such as never was yet, never shall be again. But where the Israelites dwell, all shall be still, man and beast, not a dog shall howl; you will know at last how signal a difference the Lord makes between Egypt and Israel.

. . . Make this proclamation to the whole assembly of Israel:

. . . Each household is to choose out a yearling for its own use. Or, if there are not enough of them to eat a whole lamb, the head of the family must call in some neighbour who lives close by, so that a lamb shall not be too much for their needs. It must be a male yearling lamb . . . that you choose, with no blemish on it. These victims must be kept ready till the fourteenth day of the month, and on the evening of that day the whole people of Israel must immolate. They must take some of the blood, and smear it on the doorway, jambs and lintel alike, of the house in which the lamb is being eaten. Their meat that night must be roasted over the fire, their bread unleavened; wild herbs must be all their seasoning. No part must be eaten raw, or boiled, it must be roasted over the fire; head, feet, and entrails, all must be consumed, so that nothing remains till next day; whatever is left over, you must put in the fire and burn it. And this is to be the manner of your eating it; your loins must be girt, your feet ready shod, and every man's staff in his hand; all must be done in haste. It is the night of the Pasch, the Lord's passing by. . . . $^{\Delta}$

Then, at midnight, the Lord's stroke fell; fell on every first-born thing in the land of Egypt, whether it were the first-born of Pharaoh, where he sat on his throne, or the first-born of some captive woman where she lay in her dungeon; all the first-born, too, of their cattle. So Pharaoh and all his servants and all Egypt rose up at dead of night, and all over Egypt there was loud lament; in every house a man lay dead. And it was still night when Pharaoh sent for Moses and Aaron, and said to them, Up, out of my kingdom, you and all the people of Israel with you. . . .

So the Israelites carried away the dough in their kneading-troughs before they had time to leaven it. . . . They asked the Egyptians for gold and silver trinkets, and a great store of garments. . . . The Israelites, then, set out . . . about six hundred thousand men on the march, not reckoning in the children; and with them a mingled array of other folk, past counting; they had flocks and herds, too, and beasts of all kinds. . . . It was four hundred and thirty years since the Israelites had first dwelt in Egypt; at the end of that time, the whole muster of the Lord's people left Egypt in a single day.

. . . God did not lead them by the nearest road, the road through Philistia. . . . He took them round, instead, through the desert which borders on the Red Sea. . . . And the Lord went on before, to guide them on their journey; by day, in a pillar of cloud, by night, in a pillar of fire; he was their guide at all times. . . .

And now, when the news of their escape reached the Egyptian court, Pharaoh and his servants changed their minds about the Israelites; What madness was this, they said, to let our slaves go free! So Pharaoh harnessed his chariot, and took all his troops with him . . . and he pursued the Israelites in the hour of their triumphant escape. All Pharaoh's horses and chariots, and the whole of his army, followed close on the track of the fugitives, and came upon them where they lay encamped by the sea. . . . What fear fell upon the Israelites, how they cried out to the Lord, when they looked round at Pharaoh's approach, and saw the Egyptians close behind them!

And the Lord's word came to Moses, No need to cry to me for aid; bid the Israelites march on. And do thou, meanwhile, lift up thy staff, and stretch out thy hand over the sea, parting it this way and that, so that the Israelites can walk through the midst of the sea dry-shod. . . . And with that, God's angel, that went on before the host of Israel, moved to their rear; the pillar of cloud, too, left its place in the van and came behind them. . . . Meanwhile, Moses stretched out his hand over the sea, and the Lord cleared it away from their path. All night a fierce sirocco blew, and the Lord turned the sea into dry land, the waters parting this way and that. So the Israelites went through the midst of the sea dry-shod, with the waters towering up like a wall to right and left.

The voice of Yahweh over the waters!
Yahweh over the multitudinous waters!
The voice of Yahweh in power!
The voice of Yahweh in splendour!
(Psalm 29: iii–iv. Jerusalem Bible.)

CROSSING THE RED SEA

And the Egyptians, still in pursuit, pressed on after them, all Pharaoh's mounted troops, his chariots and horsemen, driving on through the midst of the sea. It was already the first watch of the morning, when suddenly, through the pillar of fire and mist, the Lord looked down upon the Egyptians, and brought their army to its doom. He turned the wheels of their chariots aside, so that they drove through deep places, and the Egyptians began to say, Back, back! There is no facing Israel; the Lord is fighting on their side against us. Then the Lord said to Moses, Stretch out thy hand over the sea, so that its waters shall recoil on the Egyptians, on all their chariots and their horsemen. And when Moses stretched out his hand towards the sea, at early dawn, it went back to its bed, so that its waters met the Egyptians in their flight, and the Lord drowned them amid the waves. Back came the water, overwhelming all the chariots and horsemen of Pharaoh's army that had entered the sea in their pursuit; not a man escaped. But the sons of Israel made their way through the midst of the sea where it had parted, its waters towering like a wall to right and left.

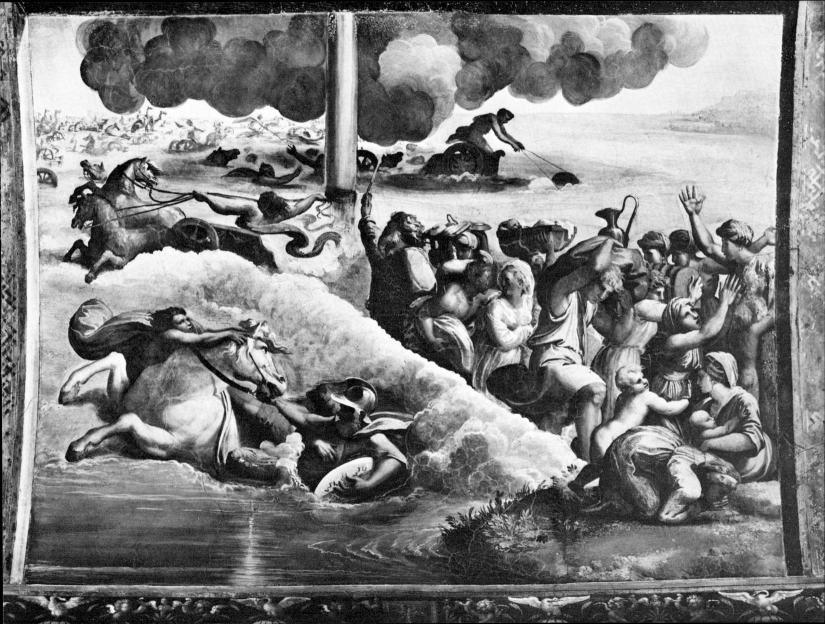

Then Moses and the Israelites sang praise to the Lord, and this was their song: A psalm for the Lord, so great he is and so glorious; horse and rider hurled into the sea! . . .

Hereupon Mary the prophetess, Aaron's sister, went out with a tambour in her hand, and all the women-folk followed her, with tambour and with dances, and took up from her the refrain, A psalm for the Lord, so great he is and so glorious; horse and rider hurled into the sea!

It was now the fifteenth day of the second month since they had left Egypt, and the Israelites, one and all, were loud in their complaints against Moses and Aaron. It would have been better, they told them, if the Lord had struck us dead in the land of Egypt, where we sat down to bowls of meat, and had more bread than we needed to content us. Was it well done to bring us out into this desert, and starve our whole company to death? But the Lord said to Moses, I mean to rain down bread upon you from heaven.

△Evening came, and brought with it a flight of quails, that settled in every part of the camp. And at morning, all about the camp, dew was lying; dew that covered the earth's surface, there in the desert, powdered fine as if it had been brayed by a pestle, lying on the ground like hoar-frost. The Israelites could not tell what it was when they went to look at it; Man-hu, they said to one another, What is it? And Moses told them, This is the bread which the Lord has sent for your eating. And this is the command the Lord gives you; everyone is to satisfy his needs; a gomor a head is the measure he is to take up, just so much for each person living in his tent.

When the sixth day came, they gathered a double allowance of two gomors a head. And when this was reported to Moses . . . he told them, Why, that is the direction the Lord has given us. Tomorrow is the sabbath, a day of rest consecrated to the Lord. . . .

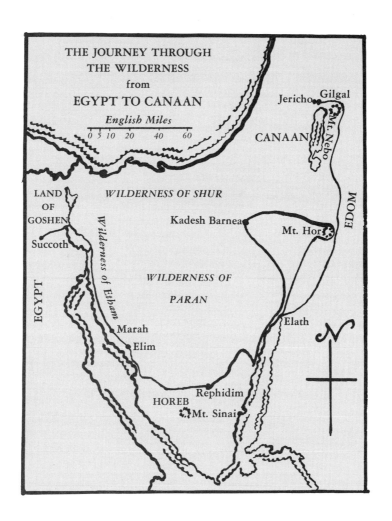

THE JOURNEY THROUGH
THE WILDERNESS
from
EGYPT TO CANAAN

English Miles

0 5 10   20   40   60

Jericho Gilgal

Mt. Nebo

CANAAN

WILDERNESS OF SHUR

LAND
OF
GOSHEN

Kadesh Barnea

EDOM

Mt. Hor

Succoth

Wilderness of Etham

EGYPT

WILDERNESS OF

PARAN

Elath

Marah

Elim

N

Rephidim

HOREB

Mt. Sinai

The wilderness and the solitary place
shall be glad . . . the desert shall rejoice,
and blossom as the rose.
. . . for in the wilderness shall waters
break out, and streams in the desert.
And the parched ground shall become a
pool, and the thirsty land springs
of water. . . .
And the ransomed of the LORD shall
return, and come to Zion with songs. . . .
(Isaiah 35: i, vi–vii, x. Authorized
Version.)

MOSES STRIKES WATER

Then the whole people of Israel left the desert of Sin, moving on from stage to stage as the Lord directed them, and encamped at Rephidim. But here they had no water to drink, so they turned upon Moses crying out, We have nothing to drink; find water for us. . . . Moses had recourse to the Lord; What can be done with them? he asked. A little more of this, and they will begin stoning me. So the Lord bade Moses march out at the head of the people, taking some of the elders of Israel with him; and as he went, he was to carry in his hand the staff which he had used to smite the river. I will meet thee, he said, at the rock of Horeb; thou hast but to smite that rock, and water will flow out of it, to give the people drink. All this Moses did, with the elders of Israel to witness it. . . .

The third new moon was rising since they left the land of Egypt, on the day when the Israelites reached the wilderness of Sinai . . . pitching their tents there in full view of the mountain. Here Moses went up to meet God, and the voice of God came to him from the mountain. . . . The time has come now when I mean to visit thee, wrapped in a dark cloud, so that all the people may hear me talking with thee, and obey thee without question henceforward.

And now the third day had come. Morning broke, and all at once thunder was heard, lightning shone out, and the mountain was covered with thick mist; loud rang the trumpet-blast, and the people in the camp were dismayed. But Moses brought them out from the camp itself to meet the Lord, and they stood there close by the spurs of the mountain. The whole of mount Sinai was by now wreathed in smoke, where the Lord had come down with fire about him, so that smoke went up as if from a furnace; it was a mountain of terrors. Louder yet grew the noise of the trumpet, longer its blast; and then Moses spoke to the Lord, and the Lord's voice was heard in answer.

And now God spoke all these words which follow. I, the Lord, am thy God, he said; I, who rescued thee from the land of Egypt, where thou didst dwell in slavery.

Thou shalt not defy me by making other gods thy own. Thou shalt not carve images, or fashion the likeness of anything in heaven above, or on earth beneath, or in the waters at the roots of earth, to bow down and worship it. I, thy God, the Lord Almighty, am jealous in my love; be my enemy, and thy children, to the third and fourth generation, shall make amends; love me, keep my commandments, and mercy shall be thine a thousandfold.

Thou shalt not take the name of the Lord thy God lightly on thy lips; if a man uses that name lightly, the Lord will not acquit him of sin.

Remember to keep the sabbath day holy. Six days for drudgery, for doing all the work thou hast to do; when the seventh day comes, it is a day of rest, consecrated to the Lord thy God. . . .

Honour thy father and thy mother; so thou shalt live long to enjoy the land which the Lord thy God means to give thee.

Thou shalt do no murder.

Thou shalt not commit adultery.

Thou shalt not steal.

Thou shalt not bear false witness against thy neighbour.

Thou shalt not covet thy neighbour's house, or set thy heart upon thy neighbour's wife, or servant or hand-maid or ox or ass or anything else that is his.

And the Lord said to Moses, Come up to the mountain and abide with me there; I have still to give thee tablets of stone on which I have written down the law and the commandments thou are to teach them. . . . So Moses climbed higher up the mountain, into the heart of the cloud; for forty days and forty nights the mountain was his home.

. . . the commandment is a lamp, and
the law a light, and reproofs of
instruction are the way of life: . . .
(Proverbs 6: xxiii. Douay.)

MOSES RECEIVES THE LAW

Then, at the end of all this converse with Moses on mount Sinai, the Lord gave him two stone tablets, with laws inscribed on them by the very finger of God.

△Meanwhile, finding that Moses' return from the mountain was so long delayed, the people remonstrated with Aaron. Bestir thyself, they said; fashion us gods, to be our leaders. We had a man to lead us, this Moses, when we came away from Egypt; but there is no saying what has become of him. Take out the gold ear-rings, said

Aaron, that your wives and sons and daughters wear, and bring them to me. The people, then, brought him their ear-rings as he had bidden them, and he melted down what they had given him and cast them into the figure of a calf. And all cried out, Here are thy gods, Israel, the gods that rescued thee from the land of Egypt. . . .

Can man make his own gods?
(Jeremiah 16: xx. Jerusalem Bible.)

THE GOLDEN CALF

. . . Moses came down from the mountain, carrying in his hand the two tablets of the law, with writing on either side, God's workmanship. . . . And now, as the noise of shouting reached him, Joshua [who waited on Moses] said to Moses, I hear the cry of battle in the camp. No, said he, this is no sound of triumph or of rout; it is the sound of singing that I hear. Then they drew nearer the camp, and he saw the calf standing there, and the dancing. And so angry was he that he threw down the tablets he held, and broke them against the spurs of the mountain. . . .

. . . Then he took the calf they had made and threw it on the fire, and beat it into dust; this dust he sprinkled over water, which he made the Israelites drink.

And now a new message came to Moses from the Lord, March on, then, with the people that has followed thee from Egypt; make thy way hence to the land I promised

Abraham, Isaac and Jacob should be the home of their race. I am ready to send an angel who will go before thee. . . . But I will not go with thee myself, stiff-necked people as thou art, or I might be moved to destroy thee on the way.

The people, on hearing this bitter reproach, went mourning. . . .

To fear the LORD is the beginning
of wisdom.
(Psalm 110: x. Grail.)

THE PILLAR OF CLOUD

Moses, too, removed his tent, and pitched it far off, away from the camp, calling it, The tent which bears witness to the covenant; to this, all who had disputes to settle must betake themselves, away from the camp. And when Moses repaired to this tent of his, all the people rose up and stood at the doors of their own tents, following Moses with their eyes till he went in.

And, once he was within the tent that bore witness of the covenant, the pillar of cloud would come down and stand at the entrance of it, and there the Lord spoke with Moses, while all watched the pillar of cloud standing there, and rose up and worshipped, each at his own tent door. Thus the Lord spoke with Moses face to face, as a man speaks to his friend.

After this the Lord said to him, Carve two tablets of stone, like those others, and I will write on them the same words as I wrote on the tablets thou didst break. . . . So Moses carved two tablets of stone, like the others; and he rose at dawn and went up mount Sinai at the Lord's bidding, with the tablets in his hand.

And the Lord answered, Here is my covenant, to which I am pledged in the presence of you all. I will do such marvels as were never yet seen on earth by any nation; the people among whom thou dwellest shall see for themselves what the Lord can do, and be terrified at the sight. Thy part is to keep all the commandments I am now giving thee.

Then the Lord said to Moses, Put these words in writing, as terms of the covenant I am making with thee and with Israel. So, for forty days and nights, without food or drink, he remained there with the Lord, and he wrote down on the tablets the ten precepts of the covenant.

. . . for my thoughts are not your thoughts,
my ways not your ways—it is Yahweh
who speaks.
Yes, the heavens are as high above earth
as my ways are above your ways, my
thoughts above your thoughts.
(Isaiah 55: viii–ix. Jerusalem Bible.)

MOSES WITH THE LAW

Moses came down, after this, from mount Sinai, bearing with him the two tablets on which the law was written; and his face, although he did not know it, was all radiant after the meeting at which he had held speech with God. The sight of that radiance made Aaron and the sons of Israel shrink from all near approach to him. . . .

And now Moses called the whole assembly of the Israelites into his presence, and told them, Here are the Lord's commands. . . . If any of you is a skilled craftsman . . . let him come forward. . . . There is a tabernacle to be made, with its covering and its canopy . . . an ark with poles to carry it, a throne over it, and a veil to hang in front of it; a table . . . a lamp-stand . . . an altar for offering incense . . . an altar for burnt sacrifice. . . .

. . . All alike began making their contributions to the Lord, with readiness and devotion of heart, to help build the tabernacle that should bear record of him. Whatever was needed . . . men and women made haste to give; armlets and ear-pendants, rings and bracelets; all the gold ware they had was set apart to be given to the Lord. And whoever had thread of blue or purple or scarlet twice-dyed . . . rams' fleeces . . . or skins . . . or silver, or bronze, offered them to the Lord. . . . All alike . . . devoutly brought their gifts, so as to speed on the work. . . .

And now Moses appointed Beseleel . . . filled with . . . divine spirit . . . wise, adroit, and skilful in every kind of craftsmanship . . . in gold, silver, bronze, and carved stone work, and carpenter's work . . . Oöliab, too . . . endowed with skill, to carry out woodwork, and tapestry, and embroidery. . . .

And so the work was begun, by Beseleel, and Oöliab . . . and trained workmen who had been endowed by the Lord with skill and had offered their services freely. . . .

. . . To carry out the fashioning of the tabernacle . . . these skilful workmen made ten curtains, of twisted linen thread, embroidered with . . . blue and purple and scarlet . . . joined five of these to each other, and the remaining five in the same way . . . with loops of blue cord, and . . . fifty gold clasps, to catch the loops so as to make a single tent of them with coverings of goats' hair, to protect the tapestry . . . a canopy, too, over the tabernacle, of rams' fleece dyed red, and another canopy over that of skins dyed violet. They made upright frames, too, of acacia wood with silver sockets to support the tabernacle . . . five poles of acacia wood, to hold the frames together on one side of the tabernacle . . . five on the opposite side . . . the sockets of silver and rings of gold through which the poles could pass. . . . They made a veil . . . embroidered with blue, purple and scarlet. . . .

Beseleel . . . made an ark of acacia wood . . . and gave it a covering and a lining of pure gold. . . . He made poles of acacia wood, gilded over, and passed them through . . . rings on the side of the ark, so as to carry it. He made a throne, too, or shrine, of pure gold . . . two cherubs of pure beaten gold . . . overshadowed it with their out-spread wings. . . . He made a table . . . with appurtenances . . . cups and bowls, goblets and censers; pure gold must be used whenever libations were poured out. . . . He made a lamp-stand . . . with lamps . . . snuffers and trays for the burnt wick. . . . The whole weight of the lamp-stand . . . was a talent of gold. . . . He made an altar . . . for burning incense . . . another . . . for burnt sacrifice. . . .

. . . On the first day of the first month, in this second year of wandering, the tabernacle was set up. . . . Moses . . . put the tablets of the law in the ark . . . and fixed the throne above it. Then, bringing the ark into the tabernacle, he spread the veil in front of it. . . . He put down the table, and . . . set out the consecrated loaves. . . . Opposite the table, he found a place for the lamp-stand. . . . And before the veil, still under the tabernacle roof, he placed the golden altar on which . . . he burnt incense made from spices. . . . By the door . . . must stand the altar for burnt-sacrifice. . . .

. . .△ When all was done, a cloud covered the tabernacle, and it was filled with the brightness of the Lord's presence. . . . Whenever the cloud lifted from the tabernacle, the Israelites would muster and . . . march, and while it hung there, they halted . . . divine cloud by day . . . divine fire by night. . . .*

[* See Appendix I.]

And now, hard put to it [again] for want of water, the people made common cause against Moses and Aaron, rebelling against their authority. Better for us, they said, if we had died when our brethren died, by the Lord's visitation! Why must you call the Lord's people out into a desert that is death to us and to our cattle? Why must you take us away from Egypt, and bring us out to this sorry place we cannot cultivate? Figs and grapes and pomegranates it yields none, and we have no water, even, to drink.

At this, when they had broken up the gathering, Moses and Aaron went into the tabernacle that bore record of the covenant, and there cast themselves down to earth in entreaty. Lord God, they said, listen to the plea made by this people of thine, and open to them thy store-house of fresh water, to content them and put an end to their complaints! Then the bright presence of the Lord was revealed to them; and the Lord said to Moses, Take thy rod with thee, and do thou and thy brother Aaron gather all the people together. Before their eyes, lay thy command upon the rock here, and it will yield water. This water thou bringest out of the rock will suffice to give drink to the whole multitude, and to their cattle. So Moses took up the rod, there in the Lord's presence, as he was bidden, and they made the people gather before the rock.△ Listen to me he said, faithless rebels: are we to get you water out of this rock? Twice Moses lifted his hand, and smote the rock with his rod; whereupon water gushed out in abundance, so that all the people and their cattle had enough to drink. But the Lord said to Moses and Aaron, Why did you not trust in me, and vindicate my holiness in the sight of Israel? It will not be yours to lead this multitude into the land I mean to give them.*

. . . To this Moses made answer, O God, art not thou Lord of every spirit that breathes? And wilt thou not find this people a ruler, who shall lead them to and fro, marching at their head? Must the people of the Lord go untended, like sheep without a shepherd? And the Lord said to him, Make choice of Joshua, the Son of Nun, a man endowed with high gifts; lay thy hand upon him, and bid him stand forth before . . . the whole assembly. There, in the sight of all, give him thy last charge, and share with him that dignity which is thine, so that all Israel may learn to obey him. . . . So Moses did as the Lord had bidden him. . . .

. . . The Lord said to Moses. Climb this mountain of Abarim (that is, of the Further Side; it is the same as mount Nebo, in the Moabite country opposite Jericho), and view the land of Canaan, which I mean to give the sons of Israel for their own. On that mountain thou art to die.

And so Moses went up from the Moabite plain on to mount Nebo. . . . And the Lord shewed him all the territory of Gad right up to Dan, and all Nephthali, and the country Ephraim and Manasse were to hold, and the whole land of Judah, with the sea coast for its frontier; the south, too, and the plain that stretches from Jericho, among its palm trees, up to Segor. This, the Lord told him, is the land of which I spoke to Abraham, Isaac and Jacob, promising to give it to their race. I have granted thee the sight of it; enter it thou mayest not.

There, then, in the land of Moab, Moses died, the Lord's servant, still true to the Lord's bidding. And there the Lord buried him . . . but where his tomb is, remains to this day unknown. He was a hundred and twenty years old when he died, and still his eyes had not grown dim, and his teeth stood firm. And the sons of Israel mourned for him thirty days, there in the plains of Moab.

. . . And Joshua . . . full of the gift of wisdom since Moses laid hands on him, took command of the Israelites; and they obeyed him, as the Lord through Moses had bidden them. . . . But there was never such another prophet in Israel as Moses; what other man was the Lord's familiar, meeting him face to face?

His servant Moses dead, the Lord gave a charge to Joshua.△ . . . Now that my servant Moses is dead, he told him, it is for thee to cross yonder stream of Jordan, taking the Israelites with thee into the land I am giving them for their own. . . . Courage, then, play the man; thy task is to divide up this land between the tribes, my promised gift to their fathers. . . . Courage and a man's part, that is what I ask of thee; no room for fear and shrinking back, when the Lord thy God is at thy side wherever thou goest.

And now Joshua bade the chieftains make their way through the midst of the camp, giving the people orders to prepare themselves food; in two days' time they were to cross the Jordan and set about conquering the land which the Lord would make their home.

Fear not . . . the battle is not yours,
but GOD's.
(II Chronicles 20: xv. Revised Version.)

PRIESTS CARRYING THE ARK

When the morrow dawned, Joshua and the men of Israel moved camp . . . to the banks of the Jordan. Here they waited three days, and then the heralds went out through the midst of the camp, and made this proclamation: When you see the priests of Levi's race on the march, carrying the ark of the Lord your God, you yourselves must follow behind them, keeping it in distant view. . . .

So the people left their encampment to go across Jordan, the priests who carried the ark marching at their head. And when these began wading out, as soon as their feet were under water (it was harvest time, and the Jordan had risen to the full height of its banks), the stream above them halted in its course. . . . And so the people marched on to the assault of Jericho; the priests carrying the Lord's ark, stood there with loins girt in the middle of the Jordan on dry ground, while the whole people went past over the dry bed of the stream.

On the tenth day of the first month the people left Jordan behind them, and encamped . . . east of the city of Jericho.

So the news went abroad among the kings of the Amorrhites, who dwelt on the west of Jordan, and the Canaanite kings by the coast of the open sea, that the Lord had dried up the stream of Jordan to let the Israelites go across. And now their hearts failed them, and their spirits were altogether daunted, such terror was theirs at the coming of Israel.

Already Jericho was bolted and barred against the approach of Israel, so that there was no entering or leaving it, and now the Lord promised to make Joshua master of it, with its king and all its defenders. Once a day, he said, you will march round the city walls, every man of you that bears arms, for six days together. And on the seventh day do as follows. The priests will be carrying seven trumpets, such as are used at jubilee time, and marching with these in front of the ark that bears witness of my covenant. On this day you will go round the city seven times, to the sound of the trumpets the priests are carrying. And when the trumpets blow a long blast that rises and falls, the whole people, on hearing it, must raise a loud cry; at that cry, the walls of the city will fall down flat, and each man will go in to the assault at the place where he is posted.

*The Lord GOD shall blow the trumpet,
and shall go with whirlwinds of the
south.
(Zechariah 9: xiv. Authorized Version.)*

THE WALLS OF JERICHO FALL△

Thus the six days passed, and on the seventh day they rose at dawn and went round the city seven times, as they were bidden. And when the priests were ready to blow their trumpets on the seventh journey, Joshua gave word to the whole of Israel, Now you are to shout; the Lord has put the city in your power.

Then the people cried aloud, and still the trumpets blew, till every ear was deafened by the shouting and the clangour; and all at once the walls fell down flat. Thereupon each man went to the assault where he was posted, and they took the city.

And now the Lord said to Joshua, No need for terror and shrinking back. Take thy whole strength of fighting men with thee, and set about the conquest of Hai; king and people, city and territory, I mean to put them all in thy power. . . .

So Joshua and all the fighting men set about the conquest of Hai. In one day all the citizens of Hai perished, men and women, to the number of twelve thousand. . . .

News of this was brought to all the other kings that lived west of Jordan, some in the hill country, some down on the plains, some on the coast by the shores of the open sea, or on the spurs of Lebanon. And all of them . . . made common cause against Joshua and the people of Israel; all were minded to offer a common resistance, except the people of Gabaon.

The king of Jerusalem, Adonisedec, was told of what had befallen; how Joshua had taken Hai and overthrown it . . . how the Gabaonites had gone over to Israel and become their allies. . . . So, from his palace at Jerusalem, Adonisedec sent envoys to Cham king of Hebron, Pharam king of Jerimoth, Japhia king of Lachis, and Dabir king of Eglon; Come and help me crush the Gabaonites, he said. . . . So it was that these five Amorrhite kings . . . joined their forces and encamped before Gabaon, offering battle. . . .

So Joshua came up . . . with all his fighting men, that were tried warriors; Have no fear, the Lord said to him, I am giving thee the mastery of them. . . . And the Lord threw them into confusion at the onslaught of Israel. . . .

Have you ever in your life given orders to
the morning or sent the dawn to its post,
telling it to grasp the earth by its
edges and shake the wicked out of it . . .
Can you fasten the harness of the
Pleiades, or untie Orion's bands?
Can you guide the morning star season
by season and show the Bear and its cubs
which way to go?
Have you grasped the celestial laws?
Could you make their writ run on the
earth?
(Job 38: xii–xiii, xxxi–xxxiii.
Jerusalem Bible.)

THE SUN STANDS STILL

It was on this day, when the Lord left the Amorrhites powerless before Israel's attack, that Joshua made that prayer of his to the Lord, crying out in the hearing of the people, Sun, that art setting over Gabaon, moon, that art rising in Aialon valley, stand stricken with awe. Sun and moon stood awe-struck, while the people took vengeance on its enemies. (So the words can be found written in the Book of the Upright). The sun stood in mid-heaven, and for a whole day long did not haste to its setting. Never was so long a day before or since, as that day when the Lord listened to a human prayer, and fought openly on the side of Israel.

For the sparrow hath found herself a
house, and the turtle a nest for herself
where she may lay her young ones: . . .
(Psalm 83: iv. Douay.)

THE DIVISION OF THE LAND

Thus, in fulfilment of the Lord's promise to Moses, Joshua occupied the whole country, and gave the several tribes enjoyment of their several portions. . . .

The division was made by lot, in pursuance of the command the Lord gave through Moses, among the . . . tribes. . . . (These did not include the Levites [the priestly tribe] since these were not to own territory like their brethren, but must be content with cities to live in and pasture for their beasts around them. . . .) The Israelites, then, set about the task of dividing up the land, as the Lord through Moses had bidden them. . . . And the land was at peace.*

[* *See Appendix II.*]

There was a man once called Elcana. . . . He had two wives, one called Anna, the other Phenenna, and this Phenenna had borne him sons, whereas Anna was childless. . . . Why had the Lord denied her motherhood? Not least, the jealousy of Phenenna made it hard to bear; Anna must be maliciously taunted with her childlessness; year after year, when they went up to the Lord's temple [at Silo] for the feast, it was ever the same. In tears she sat, with no heart for eating. . . .

Once, on such a visit to Silo, when eating and drinking was done, Anna rose up from her place and went to the temple door, where the priest Heli was sitting. Sad at heart, she prayed to the Lord with many tears, and made a vow: Lord of hosts, if thou wilt . . . keep this handmaid of thine ever in remembrance, and grant her a son, then he shall be my gift to the Lord all his life long. . . .

And the Lord bethought him of Anna, when next Elcana took her to his bed; so, in due time, she conceived and bore him a son. The name she gave him was Samuel, in token that he was a gift she had won from the Lord. . . .

She . . . nursed her child till he was weaned. And now that he needed her no longer, she took him with her to the Lord's house in Silo . . . and . . . brought the boy to Heli. . . . Anna cried out, Listen, my lord! . . . My prayer was for a son, the boy whom thou seest. . . . And the Lord granted my request; and now, in my turn, I make a grant of him to the Lord, a grant that shall be long as his life.

. . . Samuel had begun to minister in the Lord's presence, girded, though still a boy, with the linen mantle. Every year, his mother made him a little tunic, and brought it with her when she came up with her husband on feast-days for the yearly sacrifice. . . . And evermore, boy though he was, Samuel rose higher in the Lord's favour.

Heli was now a man of great age, but tales reached him of the exactions his sons made from the Israelites; how they mated, too, with the women that kept watch at the tabernacle door. . . . A messenger from the Lord came to Heli. . . . I chose Levi among all the tribes of Israel to hold the priestly office. . . . And now you spurn the due ordering of sacrifice and oblation in my sanctuary. . . . Thou shalt see a rival in my sanctuary. . . . I will find myself a priest that shall be a faithful interpreter of my mind and will.

One night, Heli lay down to rest where he was wont to lie, his eyes dim now with age and sightless, and Samuel was asleep, there in the Divine presence, where God's ark was, with the sacred lamp still burning. And the Lord's call came to Samuel. I am coming, he answered; then ran to find Heli, and said, I am here at thy summons. Nay, said he, I never summoned thee; go back and lie down again. So back he went, and fell asleep. Then the Lord called Samuel again, and again he rose up and went to Heli, to answer his summons. But still no summons had been given, and he must go back to sleep again. . . . Till then, Samuel was a stranger to the divine voice; the Lord had not made any revelation to him. But when a third time the persistent call came, and Samuel went to Heli, still ready at his command, Heli recognized at last whose voice it was the boy had heard. Go back to sleep, he told Samuel; and if the voice comes again, do thou answer, Speak on, Lord; thy servant is listening. And Samuel went back to his bed and fell asleep.

And the Lord came to his side, and stood there waiting. Then, as before, he called him twice by name; and Samuel answered, Speak on, Lord, thy servant is listening. And this was the Lord's message to Samuel: See if I do not bring on Israel such a doom as shall ring in the ears of all that hear of it. For Heli it shall bring fulfilment of all the threats I have uttered against his clan; from first to last, they shall be accomplished. Warning . . . I gave him, I would pass eternal sentence on that clan of his, for his sons' wickedness that went ever unchecked; and now I have taken an oath against all his line, sacrifice nor offering shall ever atone for their sin.

Samuel slept on till morning, when it was time for him to open the doors of the Lord's house; and fear withheld him from telling Heli of his vision. Then he heard the voice of Heli calling, Samuel, my son Samuel! I am ready at thy command, said he. And Heli asked him, What message is it the Lord has sent thee? May the Lord give thee thy due of punishment, and more than thy due, if thou hidest from me any word of the message that was given thee. Thereupon Samuel told him all that was said, keeping nothing back from him. It is the Lord, answered he, that has spoken; let him do his will.

Samuel grew up, still enjoying the Lord's favour, and no word he spoke went unful-filled, so that he became known all over Israel . . . as the Lord's true prophet. After this revelation made to Samuel in Silo, the Lord continued to reveal himself there, as he had promised; and when Samuel spoke, all Israel listened.

In his old age . . . the elders of Israel met Samuel at Ramatha; Thou hast grown old, they said to him, and thy sons do not follow in thy footsteps. Give us a king, such as other nations have, to sit in judgement over us. Little it liked Samuel, this demand for a king to be their judge; but when he betook himself to the Lord in prayer, the Lord said to him, Grant the people all they ask of thee. It is my rule over them they are casting off, not thine. It has ever been the same, since the day when I rescued them from Egypt; me they will ever be forsaking, to worship other gods. . . . Grant their request, but put thy protest on record; tell them what rights their king will claim, when they have a king to rule over them.

In answer, then, to their request for a king, Samuel told the people . . . When you have a king to reign over you, he will claim the rights of a king. He will take away your sons from you, to drive his chariots; he will need horsemen, and outriders for his teams; regiments, too, with commanders and captains to marshal them, ploughmen and reapers, armourers and wheelwrights. It is your daughters that will make his per-fumes, and cook for him, and bake for him. . . . You will be his slaves.

But Samuel could not gain the ear of the people; That will not serve, they cried out; a king, we must have a king!

There was a Benjamite in those days . . . and he had a son named Saul, a fine figure of a man, none finer in Israel; he was a head and shoulders taller than any of his fellow-countrymen.

And now Samuel took out his phial of oil, and poured it out over Saul's head; then he kissed him, and said, Hereby the Lord anoints thee to be the leader of his chosen people; thine it shall be to deliver them from the enemies that hedge them round.

. . . Once he was firmly established on the throne of Israel, Saul carried war into the territory of his enemies . . . and everywhere he won victories. . . . But Samuel reminded Saul, It was the Lord that gave me commission to anoint thee king of his people Israel; to his voice thou must needs listen. And this is the message that comes to thee from the Lord of hosts; I have not forgotten how Amalec treated the Israelites, standing in their path when they were on the way here from Egypt. This, then, is thy errand, to destroy Amalec and all his domains, granting no pardon, coveting no plunder, but slaying man and woman, child and infant at the breast, camel and ass. Whereupon Saul summoned all his men to arms. . . . He captured Agag, the Amalecite king, but although he put all the common folk to the sword, he and his army spared Agag; spared, too, the best of the flocks and herds, the choicest garments, the fattest rams; they would not destroy anything that was precious.

And the Lord's word came to Samuel, I repent, now, of having made Saul king of Israel; he has played me false, and left my command unfulfilled. . . . At early dawn Samuel rose up, resolved to find Saul that same morning; Saul . . . had . . . made his way to Galgala. When Samuel reached it, he found Saul offering the Lord burnt-sacrifice, out of the first-fruits of the plunder. . . .

May I tell thee, asked Samuel, the message the Lord has given me in the night? . . .
. . . The Lord anointed thee king of Israel, and sent thee on an errand. . . . How is it thou didst not obey the Lord's command? Why didst thou fall to plundering . . . ? Thinkest thou the Lord's favour can be won by offering him sacrifice and victim, instead of obeying his divine will? . . . Thou hast revoked thy loyalty to the Lord, and he thy kingship.

Then Saul confessed to Samuel, I have sinned. . . . Grant that sin forgiveness. . . . But now the Lord said to Samuel, What, still lamenting over Saul? I have cast him off; he is to be king of Israel no longer. Come, put oil in that phial of thine, and go on an errand for me to Jesse of Bethlehem; in one of his sons I have looked myself out a King.

Thereupon Samuel did as the Lord bade him; and when he reached Bethlehem, the elders of the city greeted him in alarm, asking whether his coming boded well for them. Yes, he told them, I have come to offer the Lord sacrifice. . . . As soon as they entered the house,* his eye fell on Eliab, and he said, Here stands the Lord's choice. . . . But the Lord warned Samuel, Have no eyes for noble mien or tall stature. . . . Not where man's glance falls, falls the Lord's choice; men see but outward appearances, he reads the heart. Then Jesse called Abinadab, and brought him into Samuel's presence; but, No, said he, this is not the Lord's choice; then Samma, but he said, No, not this one either. Seven sons of his did Jesse thus present before Samuel, but none of these, he was told, had the Lord chosen. Then Samuel asked Jesse whether these were all, and he answered, One still remains, the youngest, herding the sheep. Send for him, answered Samuel; we must not sit down till he comes.

* "The Latin version here assumes that Samuel had told Jesse the meaning of his errand." (Knox Bible, I Kings 16:viii, footnote)

A man's heart deviseth his way: but the
LORD directeth his steps.
(Proverbs 16: ix. Authorized Version.)

THE ANOINTING OF DAVID△

And Jesse sent and fetched him, red-cheeked, fair of face, pleasant of mien. And now the Lord said, Up, anoint him; this is my choice. Whereupon Samuel took out the phial of oil and anointed him then and there in his brethren's presence; and on him, on David, the spirit of the Lord came down, ever after that day.

Meanwhile the Lord's spirit passed away from Saul; instead, at the Lord's bidding, an evil mood came upon him that gave him no rest. God sends thee an ill mood, his servants told him, to disquiet thee. . . . Shall we go and find some skilful player on the harp, to relieve thee . . . by his music? . . . Thereupon a message went out from Saul to Jesse, There is a son of thine, David, that looks after thy sheep; send him to me. . . . Thus it was that David met Saul and entered his service; and became his armour-bearer, so well Saul loved him. . . . And whenever Saul was taken with this evil mood of his, David would fetch his harp, and play; whereupon Saul was comforted and felt easier, till at last the evil mood left him.

. . . The Philistines had a champion; a bastard born, that was called Goliath of Gath. His height was six cubits and a span; he wore a helmet of bronze and a breastplate of mail, this too made of bronze, and weighing five thousand sicles; greaves of bronze on his legs, and a shield of bronze to guard his shoulders. As for his spear, it had a shaft as big as a weaver's beam, with an iron head that weighed six hundred sicles; and a man went before to carry his armour for him.

Such a man confronted the ranks of Israel, crying out, What need to come here armed for battle? Here am I, champion of the Philistines; do you, that wear Saul's livery, choose out one of yourselves to meet me in single combat. If he is a match for me, and can strike me down, we will accept your rule; if I have the mastery, and he falls, you shall accept Philistine rule, and become our subjects instead.

When the Philistine had already been coming out from the ranks and confronting the Israelites for forty days together, it chanced that Jesse sent his son David on an errand. Here is a bushel of flour, said he, and ten loaves; take them with all speed to thy brethren in the camp. . . .

So David left all the gifts he had brought with him in the care of the baggage-master, and ran to the field of battle, to ask how his brethren fared. Even as he spoke, out came the champion of the Philistine cause, Goliath . . . and David heard him repeat his customary challenge.

There is nothing here, he said, to daunt any man's spirits; I . . . will go and do battle with the Philistine.

DAVID AND GOLIATH

Why then, said Saul, go, and the Lord be with thee. Then he made David wear his own armour, put a helmet of bronze on his head, and a breastplate round him; and David, as he girded on a sword over his armour, tried whether he had strength to walk in this unwonted array. Nay, he told Saul, I cannot walk, so clad; it was never my wont. So he disarmed, and took nothing but the staff he ever carried, and five smooth stones, which he picked out from the river-bed and put in his shepherd's wallet, and a sling in his hand; and so he went out to meet the Philistine.

The Philistine, with his armour-bearer going before him, came ever nearer on his way, and looked at David with contempt; here was a boy, red-cheeked and fair of face. . . . Nay, said David, though thou comest with sword and spear and shield to meet me, meet thee I will, in the name of the Lord of hosts . . . this day the Lord will give me the mastery; I will strike thee down, and cut off thy head.

By now, the Philistine had bestirred himself, and was coming on to attack David at close quarters; so, without more ado, David ran towards the enemy's lines, to meet him. He felt in his wallet, took out one of the stones, and shot it from his sling, with a whirl so dexterous that it struck Goliath on his forehead; deep in his forehead the stone buried itself, and he fell, face downwards, to the earth. Thus David overcame the Philistine with sling and stone, smote and slew him. No sword he bore of his own, but he ran up and took the Philistine's own sword from its sheath, where he lay, and with this slew him, cutting off his head.

As for David, he brought Goliath's head back with him to Jerusalem, and laid up the armour in his tent.

. . . When David returned from slaying the Philistine, the women who came out from every part of Israel to meet Saul, singing and dancing merrily with tambour and cymbal, matched their music with the refrain, By Saul's hand a thousand, by David's ten thousand fell.

. . . David defeated the Philistines and brought their pride low. . . .

David won renown, too, on his way back from the conquest of Syria, by defeating eighteen thousand men in the Valley of the Salt-pits. . . . And still the Lord protected David in all his enterprises.*

It was a long struggle between Saul's line and David's; but ever the fortunes and power of David grew, while the cause of Saul became daily weaker.

. . . All the tribes . . . rallied to David at Hebron; We are kith and kin of thine, they said . . . and there, at Hebron, in the Lord's presence, David made a covenant with them, and they anointed him king of Israel.

Your lips are a scarlet thread and
your words enchanting.
Your cheeks, behind your veil, are halves
of pomegranate....
Your two breasts are two fawns,
twins of a gazelle, that feed among
the lilies.
(Song of Songs 4: iii, v. Jerusalem Bible.)

DAVID AND BATHSHEBA

And now spring returned, the time when kings march out to battle; and David sent Joab [his general], with other servants of his and the whole army of Israel, to lay waste the Ammonite country and besiege Rabba, while he himself remained at Jerusalem. One day, he had risen from his mid-day rest, and was walking on the roof of his palace, when he saw a woman come up to bathe on the roof of a house opposite, a woman of rare beauty. So the king sent to enquire who she was, and was told that it was Bathsheba, wife of Urias the Hethite. Thereupon he sent messengers to bring her to him; she came, and he mated with her, and as soon as she was cleansed from her defilement, back she went to her home. Then finding she had conceived, she sent the news of her conception to David.

. . . David wrote a letter to Joab, which he despatched by Urias himself; and this was its purport, You are to find a place for Urias in the first line, where the fighting is bitterest; there leave him unaided, to die by the enemy's hands. So, when he next made an assault upon the city, Joab gave Urias the post where he knew the defenders were strongest; and some of these made a sally against Joab's men, killing Urias and other of David's men besides. . . .

When Urias' wife [Bathsheba] heard that he was dead, she mourned for him; her mourning over, David sent and fetched her to his palace, wedded her and had a son by her. But meanwhile David's act had earned the Lord's displeasure.

. . . The Lord sent [the prophet] Nathan on an errand to David; and this was the message he brought him. There were two men that lived in the same town, one rich, one poor. The rich man had flocks and herds in great abundance; the poor man had nothing except one ewe lamb which he had bought and reared, letting it grow up in his house like his own children, share his own food and drink, sleep in his bosom; it was like a daughter to him. The rich man was to entertain a friend, who was on his travels; and, to make a feast for this foreign guest, he would take no toll of his own flocks and herds; he robbed the poor man of the one lamb that was his, and welcomed the traveller with that. David, burning with indignation at the wrong, said to Nathan, As the Lord is a living God, death is the due of such a man as this; for this cruel deed of his, he shall make compensation fourfold. And Nathan said to David, Thou art the man.*

Then David said to Nathan, I have sinned against the Lord. . . .

* David had many wives.

So Nathan went home, and now the little son Urias' wife had borne to David was struck down by the Lord, and no hope was left for him. . . . After six days, the child died. . . . Then David comforted his wife Bathsheba, and took her to his bed; and she bore him a son whom he called Solomon. Him the Lord loved, and sent word by the prophet Nathan that he was to be called The Lord's Favourite, in proof of his great love.

. . . All the tribes of Israel rallied to David at Hebron. We are kith and kin of thine, they said. . . . He was thirty years old when his reign began, and it lasted forty years; for seven and a half years over Judah only, with its capital at Hebron, then for thirty-three more years over Israel and Judah both, with its capital at Jerusalem.

When David . . . marched on Jerusalem . . . the defenders of it told him, Thou shalt never make thy way in here. But take it he did, the keep of Sion that is called David's Keep.

. . . David's renown was noised abroad everywhere, and the Lord struck terror of him into all the nations' hearts.*

These are the words of David's last psalm. Thus speaks David, son of Jesse, thus speaks the man whom the God of Jacob swore to anoint. . . .

[* See Appendix III.] Note. David's taking of Jerusalem is out of sequence owing to the numbering of the paintings.

DAVID'S TRIUMPH△

Shall I not love thee, Lord, my rock-fastness, my bulwark, my rescuer? It is my God that brings me aid, and gives me confidence; he is my shield, my weapon of deliverance, my protector, my stronghold; he it is that preserves me and frees me from wrong. Praised be the Lord! When I invoke him I am secure from my enemies. . . .

Thou, Lord, art the lamp of my hope; thou, Lord, dost shine on the darkness about me. In thy strength I shall run well girded; in the strength of my God I will leap over a wall.

Such is my God, unsullied in his dealings; his promises are like metal tried in the fire; he is the sure defence of all who trust in him. . . . It is he that girds me with strength, he that makes me go on a smooth way, untroubled. He makes me sure-footed as the deer, and gives me the freedom of the hills; these hands, through him, are skilled in battle, these arms are a match for any bow of bronze. . . .

Then, Lord, I will give thee thanks in the hearing of all nations, singing in praise of thy name; how powerful thou art . . . towards him thou hast anointed, towards David, and David's line for ever.

(—"David's Song of Thanksgiving")

Meanwhile, Adonias, David's son by Haggith, aspired to win the throne; he must drive in state, with chariots and outriders, and fifty men to run before him; and never a word did his father say to check or challenge him. . . .

Thereupon Nathan said to Solomon's mother Bathsheba, Hast thou heard the news that Haggith's son Adonias has come to the throne, and our lord king David none the wiser? . . . So Bathsheba gained access to the king's own room, where he sat, an old, old man. . . . Low was the reverence Bathsheba made, and when the king asked what was her will, she answered, My lord, thou didst swear to me by the Lord thy God that my son Solomon should be thy heir, and succeed to thy throne; and here is Adonias already reigning, while thou, my lord king, art kept in ignorance. . . . The king took an oath: As the Lord is a living God, he who has preserved my life against all perils, my sworn word to thee, in the name of the Lord God of Israel, that thy son Solomon should be my heir and succeed to my throne, shall be fulfilled this day. And Bathsheba, bowing her face to the ground, did reverence; Unending life, said she, to my lord king David!

Then king David would have the priest Sadoc, and the prophet Nathan . . . summoned to his presence, and when these waited on him, his orders were: Take the royal troops with you, and escort my son Solomon, mounted upon my own mule, to Gihon; there let him be made king of Israel, with the priest Sadoc and the prophet Nathan to anoint him; there sound the trumpet, and make proclamation, Long live king Solomon! Then bring him back, to sit on my throne and reign instead of me; to him I commit the charge of Israel and Judah alike.

As the heavens for height, and the earth
for depth, so the mind of kings is
unsearchable.
(Proverbs 25: iii. Revised Standard
Version.)

SOLOMON ANOINTED△

Then Sadoc and Nathan . . . mounted Solomon on king David's own mule, and escorted him to Gihon; there, with a phial of oil brought out from the tabernacle, the priest Sadoc anointed Solomon king; and they sounded the trumpet, while the cry went up everywhere, Long live king Solomon! All the common folk went with him, and there was playing of flutes and great rejoicing, till earth echoed again with the noise of it.

. . . King David now summoned to his presence the clan chiefs, and the commissioners that were the king's own servants; commanders and captains, controllers of the royal property, princes and chamberlains, all that was powerful and all that was valiant in the city of Jerusalem. Rose he, and stood before them; Listen, he said. . . . I thought to have built a house, in which the ark that bears witness to the Lord's covenant should find a home, in which God's feet should have their resting-place. . . . But God warned me that it was not for me to build such a shrine for his name; I was a war-maker and a shedder of blood. . . . So the Lord himself has told me: It is Solomon, thy heir, that shall build house and court for me. . . . And do thou, my son Solomon, acknowledge ever thy father's God, serving him faithfully, serving him willingly. . . . Meanwhile, here is this house to be built, the Lord's sanctuary; on thee his choice has fallen; courage! To the task!

Then David handed over to his son Solomon the full plan of porch and temple, of store-house and parlour and inner chamber, of the throne of mercy itself. . . .

. . . or ever the silver cord be loosed, or the golden bowl be broken, or the pitcher be broken at the fountain, or the wheel broken at the cistern.
Then shall the dust return to the earth as it was: and the spirit shall return unto GOD who gave it.
(Ecclesiastes 12: vi–vii. Authorized Version.)

And now the time drew near when David must die; but first he left with his son Solomon this charge. I am going, said he, the way all mortal things go at last; do thou keep thy courage high and play the man. Hold ever true to the Lord thy God, following the paths he has shewn us, observing his ceremonies, and all those commands and awards and decrees that are contained in the law of Moses. . . .

So David was laid to rest with his fathers, and the Keep of David was his burial-place. . . .

By now, Solomon's power was firmly established, and he allied himself by marriage to the king of Egypt, whose daughter he wedded.

Great love had Solomon for the Lord, and followed the counsel of his father David, though indeed he too went to mountain shrines, to sacrifice and offer up incense. Once he had betaken himself to Gabaon, where there was a famous mountain shrine. . . . And that night the Lord appeared to him in a dream, bidding him choose what gift he would. Thou has been very merciful, answered Solomon, to my father David . . . but, Lord, what am I? No better than a little child, that has no skill to find its way back and forth. . . . Be this, then, thy gift to thy servant, a heart quick to learn, so that I may be able to judge thy people's disputes, and discern between good and ill.

The Lord listened well pleased. . . . For this request of thine, he told Solomon, thou shalt be rewarded . . . hereby I grant thee a heart full of wisdom and discernment, beyond all that went before thee or shall come after thee.

SOLOMON'S JUDGEMENT

And now two women, harlots both of them, came and stood in the royal presence. Justice, my lord! said one of them. This woman and I share a single house, and there, in her presence, I gave birth to a child; three days after my delivery, she too gave birth. We were still living together; none else was in the house but we two. Then, one night, she overlay her child as she slept, and it died. So, rising at dead of night, when all was still, she took my son from beside me, my lord, while I slept, put him in her own bosom, and her dead son in mine. In the morning, when I raised myself to give my child suck, a dead child was there; and it was not till I looked at it more closely under the full light of day that I found this was never the child I bore. And when the other woman said, No, it is thy child that is dead, mine that is alive, she persisted in answering, Thou liest; it is my child that lives, thine that is dead. Such was the angry debate they held in the king's presence.

See, said the king, it is all, My child lives and thine is dead, on the one side, and Thy child is dead and mine lives, on the other. Bring me a sword. So a sword was brought out before the king. Cut the living child in two, he said, and give half to one, half to the other. Whereupon the true mother of the living child, whose heart went out to her son, cried out, No, my lord, give her the living child; never kill it! Not so the other; Neither mine nor thine, she said, let it be divided between us. No, said the king, do not kill the living child, give it to the first; she is its mother.

A house Solomon would build, to be a shrine for the Lord's name. . . . So he made a register of seventy thousand men that should carry burdens on their backs, and eighty thousand to quarry stone in the hills; of overseers, he would have three thousand six hundred. And he sent a message to Hiram, king of Tyre: When my father David was building the palace in which he dwelt, thou didst send him planks of cedar. Do as much for me, now that I would build a temple dedicated to the Lord, the God I worship; there to burn incense of rich spices, keep hallowed loaves set forth continually, offer sacrifice at morning and evening, at sabbath and at new moon, and on all the feasts our changeless rite enjoins in the Lord's honour.

A craftsman I would have of thee, that can work skilfully in gold and silver, copper and iron, tapestry of purple and scarlet and blue; that can help the workmen my father David has left me, here in Jerusalem, carve the figures they would. Send me planks, too, of cedar and juniper and pine; I know well how deftly thy men can fell trees on Lebanon; mine shall be apprenticed to them, and cut me planks in abundance; it is a great temple, a famous temple, I would build . . .

To this Hiram [the king] wrote . . . I am sending thee a wise man and a skilful, one [also called] Hiram, that is a master of his craft. . . . Well he knows how to work in gold and silver, copper and iron, in marble and in wood, in tapestry of purple and blue, lawn and scarlet thread; to carve what carving thou wilt, and devise all that needs devising, thy craftsmen to aid him, and the craftsmen the king's grace, thy father, left thee. My lord, we are at thy service; do thou send us wheat and barley, wine and oil, as thou hast promised, and we will set about cutting the planks thou needest, on mount Lebanon. They shall be brought in rafts by sea to Joppa, and it shall be thy part to carry them to Jerusalem.

. . . this is none other but the house of
GOD, and this is the gate of heaven.
(Genesis 28: xvii. Authorized Version.)

. . . mine house shall be called an house
of prayer for all people.
(Isaiah 56: vii. Authorized Version.)

BUILDING THE TEMPLE

Solomon, then, set about the building of the Lord's house. . . . It was in the second month of his fourth year as king that he began building, and the foundations he laid for the Lord's house, using the old cubit measure, were sixty cubits long and twenty cubits wide. In front was a porch twenty cubits long, to match the width of the temple, and (a hundred and) twenty cubits high, the gilding within was of the purest gold. The main building was faced with planks of pine, that had plates of fine gold attached to them, and it had a pattern of palm branches and chains interlaced; its floor was laid in precious marble, nobly patterned. The whole building, beam and pillar and wall and doorway, was faced with none but the purest gold, and on the walls of it were carvings of cherubim.

So Judah and Israel, countless in number as the sand by the sea, ate, drank, and were merry. As for Solomon, he bore rule over all the kingdoms between the river of Palestine and the border of Egypt, enjoying the tribute they brought him and the service they did him all his life long.

Wisdom, too, God gave to Solomon, and great discernment, and a store of knowledge wide as the sand on the sea shore. . . . Three thousand parables king Solomon uttered, and of songs he made a thousand and five; and he discoursed of all the trees there are, from the cedar on Lebanon to the hyssop that grows out from the wall; and of beasts, and birds, and creeping things, and fish. From all peoples and all kings of the world, when his fame reached them, men came to take back word of Solomon's wisdom.

SOLOMON AND THE QUEEN OF SHEBA

And now Solomon was visited by the queen of Sheba. She had heard by report of the wisdom with which the Lord's favour had endowed him, and came to make trial of his powers with knotty questions. Magnificent was the retinue with which she entered Jerusalem; spices and abundant gold and precious stones were the lading of her camels. And when she met king Solomon, he told her all the secrets her heart concealed; every doubt he resolved, no question of hers but found an answer. And when she saw how wise a man he was, saw, too, the house he had built, the food that was on his table, the lodging of his servants, the order and splendour of his court, how the wine went round, and what burnt-sacrifice he offered in the Lord's temple, she stood breathless in wonder. And she said to the king, It was no false tale I heard in my own country, of all thou dost and of all the wisdom that is thine. I could not believe what they told me, without coming and seeing it for myself; and now I find that half of it was lost in the telling; here is greater wisdom, greater prosperity than all the tales that reached me. Happy thy folk, happy these servants of thine who wait ever upon thy presence and listen to thy wise words. Blessed be the Lord thy God, who, in his eternal love for Israel, has brought thee, his favourite, to the throne, given thee a king's power to do justice and to make award!

When Solomon had . . . achieved all his purpose, the Lord appeared to him a second time, as he had appeared to him once at Gabaon. I have listened to thy prayer, the Lord told him, to the suit thou hast preferred before me; and this temple thou hast built I myself have hallowed, to be the everlasting shrine of my name; never a day but my eyes shall be watching, my heart attentive here. Do thou guide thy steps, like thy father, as in my presence, with an undivided heart and steadfastly. . . .

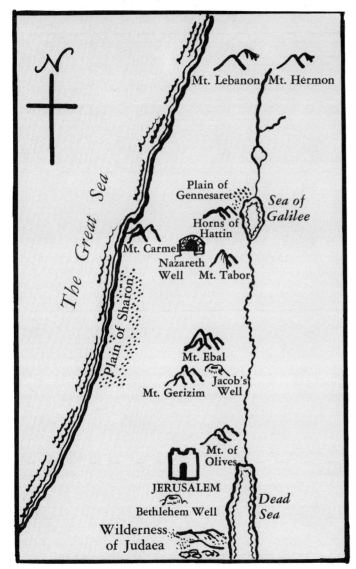

THE COUNTRY OF JESUS

JESSE
↓
David
↓
Solomon
↓
↓
Joseph△
(the husband of Mary)
of her was born   JESUS   who is called Christ

RAPHAEL'S WORKSHOP

The leader, and Raphael's right hand for both landscape and figures in the workshop, was Giulio Romano.

In 1499 when Giulio Romano was born in Rome, the city had no distinctive school of painting. The wonderful troop—Botticelli, Ghirlandaio, Signorelli, Perugino, and so on—assembled by Pope Sixtus IV, had gone, and art had almost come to a standstill until Julius II, after his election, called another and even more gifted galaxy of talent to Rome and Raphael opened his workshop; the boy Giulio would have been trusted only with the grinding of colours, preparation of plaster, and so on, but the artist developed well and Raphael is said to have loved him like a son.

Giulio Romano's figures never had the depth, the inner force of Raphael's, but his style has a thunder-and-lightning quality, often dramatic and menacing, of real grandeur and terror. This shows strongly in some of the Loggia scenes: God Dividing Light from Darkness; the cataclysmic Deluge; Moses on Sinai; and The Pillar of Cloud in the Camp.

Francesco Penni (1496–1540) joined Raphael in 1512. Penni was called *Il Fattore,* the Creator, but it seems he may have been misnamed because many critics attribute the weaker of the Loggia scenes to him, saying that he completely vitiated the conceptions of Raphael; The Creation of Eve, the scenes of Isaac with Esau and Jacob, show "dumpy proportions, plump limbs, and babyish expressions." Certainly when, after Raphael's death, Giulio Romano and Penni tried to continue the workshop, it failed.

Perino del Vaga (1501–1547) was a late-comer to the workshop, and his first work for Raphael was done in the Loggia; beginning by drawing designs for *stucchi* and *grotteschi* under Giovanni da Udine, he went on to paint some of the scenes themselves. Some say his, not Penni's, are the weaker paintings; others that some of the best are Perino's, but everyone agrees that it was he who painted the scenes from Joshua. Vasari evidently thought Perino del Vaga an important painter because he devoted a long chapter to him, but Perino seems to have made little impact on later critics. He married Penni's sister and became, as Alessandro Marabottini, the art critic, calls him, "an elegant butterfly."

Polidoro da Caravaggio (born about 1500) came to Rome when the *Loggie* were being built. The story is that he was employed at first as a bricklayer but, learning about painting, was promoted to the workshop. It seems far more likely that the boy knew he had some skill and, in order to get into Raphael's ambiance and be noticed by his painters, took any task connected with the Loggia. He was only eighteen, and there is remarkable vigour in his paintings.

Most interesting of the workshop painters seems to have been Giovanni da Udine. He joined Raphael about 1514 when he, Giovanni, was twenty-seven, not as a pupil but a fully fledged painter of still life, animals, and birds; he became Raphael's chief decorator, and it seems more than likely that he was responsible for the decorations in the Loggia—though a strong case has been made out for Peruzzi. The decorations are of extreme beauty and delicacy, and it is interesting to note that Giovanni da Udine came from a family of embroiderers.

These were a few of Raphael's team—or galaxy, as they have been called. They all dispersed after his death, most of them into oblivion.

Even in full work the workshop artists could have earned very little; there is a record of a payment of twenty-five ducats to them—about fifty of the crowns of that period—but this surely must have been a part payment. In those times, fifty ducats a year was enough for only the bare necessities of life, a hundred to a hundred and fifty enough for ease, and three hundred for luxury. Michelangelo was paid two thousand crowns for the Sistine frescoes—twenty months' work. Raphael earned thousands of crowns.

NOTES ON THE LOGGIA PAINTINGS

In the time of Raphael, people, though Catholic, did not often read the Bible, and it has been suggested that the seemingly erratic choice of the subjects of the Loggia paintings was due to the fact that this was guided by the study of Dante rather than of the Old Testament.

Dante was the forerunner or opener of the Renaissance, the first serious poet to write in Italian, not Latin, and Raphael and his assistants almost certainly read him. In the *Inferno,* Canto IV, when Christ intervenes for the souls in limbo, Dante writes:

> He drew from hence our primal parent's shade,
>> Abel his son, and Noah, nor forgot
>> Moses who gave the laws himself obey'd;
> patriarch Abraham and king David, not
>> omitting Israel, with his sire and sons
>> and Rachel, for whose sake so much he wrought
>> and many more . . . [1]

Though there is no scene in the Loggia of the murder of Abel by Cain, they are shown as children; Abraham's story is incomplete, but there is the same emphasis on Rachel, so the suggestion of Dante's influence may be true.

[1] Translated by Geoffrey L. Bickersteth.

THE BEGINNING (page 19)

There is a feeling, not only of power, but of calm and certainty in these four scenes; God is always painted in a purple mantle and one wonders if the painters of this Old Testament Jehovah knew that Canaan was "the land of the purple"; from earliest times its inhabitants had extracted from a native shellfish (murex) this most famous dye of the ancient world. It was so uncommon, so difficult to obtain, therefore so expensive . . . that purple robes were the mark of high rank.[2]

GOD SEPARATES THE ELEMENTS (page 20)

This scene is almost certainly the work of Giulio Romano.

The ancient Semites believed that the vault of the sky (the firmament) was a solid dome holding the upper waters in check; the waters of the Deluge poured down through apertures in it.[3]

CREATION OF THE SUN AND THE MOON (page 24)

In the accompanying narrative their names were deliberately omitted; the Sun and Moon, deified by all the neighbouring peoples, are here no more than lamps that light the earth and regulate the calendar.

CREATION OF THE ANIMALS (page 27)

The creatures in this scene are so endearing, so beautifully spaced and painted that it seems likely that Giovanni da Udine painted them into the picture.

[2] Werner Keller, *The Bible As History* (New York: Morrow, 1956). [3] Jerusalem Bible.

THE STORY OF ADAM AND EVE (pages 28–40)

"She is to crush thy head . . ." (page 35). The pronoun is taken to refer to Mary and
the Incarnation, and this interpretation has become current in the Church.

THE STORY OF NOAH (pages 40–54)

Here Giulio Romano's characteristics show clearly in "The Deluge," and once again Giovanni da Udine must be the painter of the animals in "The Descent from the Ark."

Archaeologists have found another story of the flood, almost identical to Noah's, in the Epic of Gilgamesh, inscribed on the eleventh of twelve clay tablets discovered among the ancient ruins of the library at Nineveh. In it is a description of a great storm, black clouds and a roaring noise, sudden darkness in broad daylight; any meteorologist recognizes this as a description of a cyclone; and "in tropical regions, the coastal areas, islands, above all alluvial river flats, are subject to a spiral type of tidal wave which leaves devastation and destruction in its wake. One such, in 1876, swept up from the Bay of Bengal and the deltas of the Ganges . . . and 215,100 people died.[4]

(Page 48) Mount Ararat is in Eastern Turkey on the borders of Russia and Iran. It is 16,000 feet high and always capped with snow. . . . For generations the people of the little village that lies at its foot have recounted the story of a mountain shepherd who was said to have seen on Ararat a great wooden ship. The findings of a Turkish expedition in 1833 seem to confirm the shepherd's story because they mention the prow of a great wooden ship which, in the summer season, stuck out of the south glacier.[5]

[4] Keller. [5] Ibid.

THE STORY OF ABRAHAM AND OF THE BURNING OF SODOM (pages   *THE FOURTH VAULT*
54–71).

(Page 55) Abraham came from Haran to Canaan, more than six hundred miles. Though it is not shown on the map (page 54), he must have had to cross the mighty river Euphrates, a considerable achievement with his huge clan of men, women, children, and flocks and herds.

(Page 55) In the narrative, Abraham's nephew Lot is suddenly called his brother; in many Eastern languages "brother" is used in its widest sense, meaning any relation.

(Page 58) "Abram" in the Hebrew signifies "a high father," but "Abraham" means "the father of the multitude."

(Page 61) Likewise "Sarai" signifies "my lady," but "Sara" absolutely "Lady." [6]

(Page 68) Sodom and Gomorrha, it has been established now, disappeared when the whole Vale of Siddim, with its cities, was plunged into an abyss, probably by a violent earthquake, and submerged by the Jordan River into what is now the Dead Sea, 1200 feet below normal sea level. This cataclysm happened about 1900 B.C., in the time of Abraham. The Dead Sea has no outlet, but the water evaporates under the hot sun, and the sea really is deadly; normal ocean water has only 4.6 percent of salt, but nothing can live in the Dead Sea because the water has 25 percent of solid ingredient, mostly sodium chloride, cooking salt—yet when one tastes it, it is more like Epsom Salt. A swimmer cannot sink in the Dead Sea, and will emerge from it coated with salt that dries white, which possibly explains Lot's wife. "When a boat is taken out on the water, and the sun is in the right direction, clearly visible in the depths below are forests preserved, or pickled, in salt. Perhaps Lot's flocks grazed under those very trees." [7]

(Page 71) ". . . became a part of his people"—i.e., gathered to his people—is synonymous with death.

[6] Douay. [7] Keller.

THE STORY OF ISAAC (pages 70–87)

(pages 70–87)

THE FIFTH VAULT

This has two of the weakest pictures: "Isaac Blesses Jacob," and "Esau Begs for a Blessing," but also has two of the finest: "Isaac, Rebecca, and Abimelech," and "God Commands Isaac." In the latter, God, in his purple mantle, has not the thunder and power of Romano's conception, but the composition, with Isaac's pose in which his staff makes a diagonal line across the painting, is exquisitely balanced, while the landscapes above and around are delicately luminous.

This vault, too, has the best decoration (repeated in the ninth, which is less damaged), with marbled window spaces and cornices painted open to the sky in which birds perch or fly, swallows—especially difficult to paint—a small huddled owl.

THE STORY OF JACOB (pages 78–101, 120–21)

"Jacob's dream" (page 88), with its simple yet intense composition, could be a re-use of a study by Raphael. The shining angels, as they mount up to God, recall the angel in "The Deliverance of Saint Peter from Prison" in the Stanza d'Eliodoro. "Laban Meets Jacob" (page 93) is a pleasing pastoral, but the sheep and goats have not the quality of Giovanni da Udine's animals—the camels in "Parting of Jacob with Laban" (page 99) are particularly hideous; it has been established, too, that these creatures were unknown in the ancient world; references to them in Genesis must have crept in later. The Old Testament camels were probably donkeys.

(Page 89) The ways of God truly can be called inscrutable: when the shocking character of Jacob is contrasted with Esau's, Jacob's cowardice with Esau's generosity (see page 101), it is hard to understand why Jacob was preferred. The women, too, were jealous and deceitful; Rebecca's deception of Isaac is hateful, and Rachel even stole her father Laban's household gods when she fled with Jacob.

THE STORY OF JOSEPH (pages 103-21)

This is one of the finest vaults. "Joseph Tells His Dream" (page 105) is so well balanced that it might again be from a drawing by Raphael. The dreams themselves are inset as small medallions high up in the pictures.

The centre of this vault shows the arms of Pope Leo X: the six gold balls of the Medici with the Pope's triple crown and crossed keys. These, and Leo's name, recur over and over again in the Loggia, obviously in homage—or flattery.

(Page 103) ". . . a coat that was all embroidery." We are so used to the "coat of many colours" that this comes as a shock; the Jerusalem Bible merely gives "a coat with long sleeves," but there is no doubt that the Israelites loved bright colours, and one of the pictures in the tomb of Beni-Hasan shows a type of coat with a wonderful red and blue pattern. Red and blue were the colours for men's wear; green seems to have been reserved for women. Pomegranates and saffron yielded a lovely yellow, madder root and safflower a fiery red, woad a heavenly blue; there was also ochre and red chalk, while the sea donated that queen of all dyes . . . purple.[8]

There is still a place in Egypt that bears Joseph's name; eighty miles south of Cairo is the fertile Faiyum with its lush gardens of oranges, mandarins, peaches, olives, and grapes; Faiyum owes these fruits to an artificial canal over two hundred miles long which brings water from the Nile to turn what would be desert into this paradise. The ancient waterway is called "Bahr Yusuf"—Joseph's canal. People say it was the Joseph of the Bible who planned it.

THE SEVENTH VAULT
(THE CENTRAL ONE)

[8] Keller.

THE STORY OF MOSES (pages 125–68)

In "Moses Brought from the Water" the baby has curly golden hair like a cherub's, which he keeps as the young shepherd in "Moses and the Burning Bush," not odd in Rome but odd for an Israelite of those times. "Crossing the Red Sea" seems especially unsuccessful compared to the drama of the flood in the painting of "The Deluge"; here the water seems solid; the pillar of cloud looks solid, too, a literal pillar, and it is coloured orange, which seems a strange choice; even the struggling horse in the foreground seems static.

(Page 134) The plagues sent to Egypt: ". . . the rivers turned to blood." Deposits from the Abyssinian lakes often colour the floodwaters a dark reddish brown . . . that might well be said to look like blood. At the time of the floods frogs and also flies sometimes multiply so rapidly that they become regular plagues on the land. Under the heading "lice" would come the dog-fly . . . cattle pest is known all over the world. The "boils" might have been the so-called Nile-heat or Nile-itch—a stinging rash that often develops into ulcers. Hailstorms are rare but not unknown in Egypt, but swarms of locusts are a typical and disastrous phenomenon in the Orient. . . . The same is true of sudden darkness when a blistering hot wind whirls up vast masses of sand in the desert until they obscure the sun. The "deaths of the firstborn" is a plague for which there is no parallel,[9] nor can it be explained why the plagues came one after the other in what seems to have been a comparatively short time.

(Page 136) "It is the night of the Pasch . . ." i.e., the Passover; though the name derives from the "passing over" of the marked houses, it is a combination of two much older festivals, both of the springtime. One was a pastoral feast, offering the first-fruit of the flock; the other, the feast of unleavened bread, was primarily agricultural, offer-

[9] Keller.

ing the first-fruit of the barley harvest. These became fused at a very early date, and, once associated with the deliverance out of Egypt of the Israelites, the rites took on new significance.[10]

(Page 143) Quails and manna: these were not miraculous but perfectly matter-of-fact occurrences. The Israelites left Egypt in spring, the time when birds migrate from Africa; from time immemorial they (the birds) have taken two routes, one via the west coast of Africa to Spain, the other by the Eastern Mediterranean to the Balkans and beyond. Quails and other birds on this eastern route must fly across the Red Sea; when they alight on the shores they are so exhausted that it is possible to pick them by the hundreds off the ground.

Of manna, the Jerusalem Bible gives: "When the coating of dew was lifted, there, on the surface of the desert, was a thing delicate and powdery. . . ." Manna is actually a secretion exuded by tamarisk trees and bushes when they are pierced by a certain type of plant louse found in Sinai.[11] The secretion falls to the ground white, but turns yellow-brown later; it is as sweet as honey. The Bible says, "When the sun waxed hot it melted away," but in fact it has to be gathered early or the ants take it. The Bedouins still collect and knead the manna into a purée.

In Christian tradition manna is a figure of the Eucharist, the spiritual food of the Church, the new Israel, on her earthly journey to the Promised Land.[12]

THE STORY OF MOSES (continued)

The quality of these four scenes, especially the pillar of cloud by Moses's tent, points to their being by Giulio Romano. Here, repeating the illusory architecture of the fifth vault, are more of Giovanni da Udine's birds—but this time these are a pair of hoopoes, a string of swans, another owl, but balanced by a swallow.

(Page 150) Aaron made the Golden Calf: it is difficult to understand—though Moses reproached him—why Aaron apparently escaped any retribution for allowing the people to lapse into this most deadly of all sins, blasphemy or idolatry. He, with Moses, was punished for a much slighter offence at the Waters of Rebellion, while one of the drivers of the oxen that drew the Ark, Ozias, was struck dead because "he put his hand on the Ark" to steady it when it was being carried over the Jordan.

(Page 166) The Ark: "I have not dwelt in a house since the day I brought up the people of Israel from Egypt. . . . I have been moving about in a tent for my dwelling. . . ." (II Samuel 7: vi, see Knox). The ark was regarded as the most venerable of Israelite objects (see above what happened to Ozias when he put his unconsecrated hand on it). Even when finally installed by David in the Temple at Jerusalem, it was always housed in a tent or tabernacle to accord with nomadic conditions of life. Even now, in the Christian ritual for the dedication of a church, in the lesson of the Mass the consecrated church is spoken of as "God's tent pitched here on earth."

(Page 167) The second striking of the rock: Moses came from the water, and water was his downfall. "This is the place called the Water of Rebellion" (Numbers 20: xiii), said the Lord of this second striking of the rock for water. At first reading of this story it is again difficult to understand the Lord's terrible punishment of Moses and

Aaron, or even to discover what was their sin, but, reading more carefully, one sees that Moses did not implicitly obey God: he was told to "lay his command upon the rock," but he smote it twice—perhaps he even lost his temper—he certainly called the people "faithless rebels"; he also said, "Are we to get you water out of this rock?" "We"—not "the Lord." It might also seem, for the moment, as if Moses wanted to show *his* power—not God's.

It is interesting that Moffat, in his translation of Numbers 20, only puts dots for these passages, which generally means that in his opinion the text is corrupt; possibly in this case it has been tampered with so as not to show Moses in a bad light.

Of this striking of the rock and water gushing out, Keller says that the Bible is once more recording a natural occurrence. The rock was limestone, which can form a smooth hard crust under which is often a spring of water. Moses had obviously got to know this unusual way of finding water when he was in exile among the Midianites, but Werner Keller does not—and probably cannot—explain how Moses knew exactly where to find it.

THE TENTH VAULT THE STORY OF JOSHUA (pages 169–82)

This is the vault which all the critics agree was painted by Perino. The paintings have a curious naïveté compared to the authority of the rest, an interlinking rhythm which, though stylish—as Perino later became—destroys the dramatic content. The Sun and Moon, in the scene where Joshua orders them to stand still, seem curiously small compared to the dominating figure of Joshua, while the naked warrior hiding under his shield is almost comically passive. In "The Division of the Land" the priest, a Levite (?), sitting beside Joshua, wears a headdress very like a mitre, and the boy in the foreground is naked. Why?

(Page 177) "The Walls of Jericho Fall": In the early years of this century a German-Austrian expedition at Jericho exposed two concentric rings of fortifications, the inner ring surrounding the ridge of the hill. They were made of sun-dried bricks . . . the inner wall about twelve feet thick throughout, the outer six feet, and about twenty-five to thirty feet high . . . a masterpiece of military defence. Later a British expedition made a remarkable discovery; when the walls were destroyed, the outer wall had fallen outwards and downwards, but the inner wall fell the opposite way—inwards; the only conclusion the archaeologists could draw was that an earthquake had shattered the city.

THE STORY OF DAVID (pages 190–209)

The painting that stands out here is "The Anointing of David [by Samuel]": the bashful boy with his shy, clumsy stance, the jealousy of the other sons of Jesse, the awe of Jesse himself, the suggestion of power in Samuel's arm as he pours the anointing oil, and the small landscape seen through the window, are beautifully balanced.

By contrast, "David and Goliath" is a muddle; the fallen figure of the giant and David standing astride him are lost in the mêlée of the fight. As I said on the first page of these notes, in the days of Raphael few people read the Bible, and probably the painter of this scene did not know that the battle between Goliath and David was "single combat."

The painting of "David's Triumph" (page 203) is a puzzling one. The head on the spear, the empty suit of armour seemed to belong to King Saul when David's soldiers paraded these through the camp, but David certainly would not have done this as he grieved bitterly for Saul and Jonathan. The painting has also been called "his triumph over the Assyrians," but in both of these victories David was still a young man. It seems more likely that this is his victorious return to Jerusalem after the defeat and death of Absalom. How David was first able to take Jerusalem, the "Keep," was, for centuries, a puzzle, but it was solved by a simple and curious story which is quoted by Dr. Keller:

> "On the east side of Jerusalem where the rock slopes down into the Kidron valley lies the 'Ain Sitti Maryam,' the 'Fountain of the Virgin Mary.' In the Old Testament it is called 'Gihon,' 'bubbler,' and it has always been the main water supply for the inhabitants of the city. The road to it goes past the remains of a small mosque and into a vault. Thirty steps lead down to a little basin in which the pure water from the heart of the rock is gathered.

THE ELEVENTH VAULT

241

"In 1867 a Captain Warren, in company with a crowd of pilgrims, visited the famous spring which, according to the legend, is the place where Mary washed the swaddling clothes of her little Son. Despite the semi-darkness Warren noticed on this visit a dark cavity in the roof, a few yards above the spot where the water flowed out of the rock. Apparently no one had ever noticed this before because when Warren asked about it nobody could tell him anything.

"Filled with curiosity, he went back to the Virgin Fountain next day equipped with a ladder and a long rope. He had no idea that an adventurous and somewhat perilous quest lay ahead of him.

"Above the spring a narrow shaft went straight up into the rock. Warren was an alpine expert and well acquainted with this type of chimney climbing. Carefully, hand over hand, he made his way upwards. After about 40 feet the shaft suddenly came to an end. Feeling his way in the darkness, Warren eventually found a narrow passage. Crawling on all-fours, he followed it. A number of steps had been cut in the rock. After some time he saw ahead of him a glimmering of light. He reached a vaulted chamber which contained nothing but old jars and glass bottles covered in dust. He forced himself through a chink in the rock and found himself in broad daylight in the middle of the city, with the Fountain of the Virgin lying far below him.

"Closer investigation by Parker, who in 1910 went from the United Kingdom under the auspices of the Palestine Exploration Fund, showed that this remarkable arrangement dated from the second millennium B.C. The inhabitants of old Jerusalem had been at pains to cut a corridor through the rock in order that in time of siege they could reach in safety the spring that meant life or death to them.

"Warren's curiosity had discovered the way which 3,000 years earlier David had used to take the fortress of Jerusalem by surprise. David's scouts must have known about this secret passage, as we can now see from a Biblical reference which was previously obscure. David says: 'Whosoever getteth up to the gutter and smiteth the Jebusites . . .' (2 Samuel 5: viii). The Authorized Version translated as 'gutter' the Hebrew word *'sinnor,'* which means a 'shaft' or a 'channel.' "13

(Page 202) "David's Song of Thanksgiving." The more one studies the life of David the more his genius emerges: mighty in war, with the courage of the lion he killed as a boy, he was also a diplomat, a builder, and yet a musician and one of the greatest poets of all time—the psalms have a beauty too often taken for granted.

He plumbed the depths of sin with his murder of Urias for the sake of his own lust for Bathsheba, and broke the law by taking her, another man's wife, to bed. He plumbed the depths, too, of sorrow, especially the bitter sorrow of the rebellion of his beloved son Absalom, who turned into an enemy and over whose death David could not even allow himself to grieve; his general, Joab, made his way into the royal lodging where David was mourning and said: "Here is a fine day's work to make all thy followers go about hanging their heads! . . . Never a thought this day for thy own captains and thy own men. . . . Bestir thyself, come out and speak to thy men. . . . I swear by the Lord, if thou dost not come out, not a man will be left to serve thy cause by nightfall."

David's six-pointed star remains the badge of the Jews—Solomon, not wishing to emulate his great father, took only five points—and David's tomb is today a place of the greatest reverence on Mount Zion.

13 Keller.

THE STORY OF SOLOMON (pages 201–20)

The scenes of "Solomon Anointed" and "Solomon's Judgement" seem to show a new, unknown artist's hand, and a poor one; the compositions are awkward, the draperies seem made of paper.

The recumbent figure in the right foreground of "Solomon Anointed" is the personification of the River Jordan; he is holding in his left hand the marsh cane symbolizing the ancient river and leaning on a tiger—so uncommon in Roman art of the period that it causes wonder as to how it came there; the first thought was that it is a symbol of the River Tigris, but that name comes from the Persian "*tigra,*" meaning an "arrow" and denoting the river's swiftness.

Tigers were later sent by Indian princes to the Roman emperors; perhaps Raphael concluded they might have been sent to Solomon among the fabulous gifts that came to him from far and wide.

"Building the Temple" and "Solomon and the Queen of Sheba" are said to be by the young Polidoro and certainly show a different spirit. The Temple painting is badly damaged, yet the drama and intensity of its figures can still be seen; in the Sheba scene, the queen is so eager that she is almost running to meet Solomon, whose rising to meet her shows great tenderness—he is already old, she very young. Once again there is a touch of naïveté—both are wearing crowns.

(Pages 212–17) Solomon's reign, which reads like a fairy tale, has yielded the archaeologists more exact truth than any other Biblical research. They have found his long-vanished seaport of Ezion Geber which was not only a port but a dockyard where Solomon's navy was built with timber brought from Tyre on eight thousand of those fabled camels. The Israelites were not a seagoing people, and Solomon sent for Phoenician shipbuilders and sailors. Above all, Ezion Geber was the centre of the copper industry; indeed, Solomon could have been called the copper and iron king;

his mines and furnaces have been found. He had, says Dr. Keller, "a flair for exploiting foreign brains and skill and turning them to his own advantage . . ." which is how the simple peasant régime of his father David grew into a first-class economic organization. This flair was also the secret of Solomon's wealth.[14]

(Page 218) In Solomon's time, a gigantic dam blocked the river Adhanat at Sheba in the then fabulous lands of southern Arabia. Rainfall collected there and the water was led off in canals which irrigated Sheba and gave it an extraordinary fertility. Sheba was the Land of Spices, one vast fairylike scented garden of the costliest spices in the world, but in 542 B.C. the dam burst and the spice gardens became desert.

[14] Ibid.

FOUR SCENES FROM THE NEW TESTAMENT (page 221)

Joseph, the husband of Mary: the force of Jewish betrothal was such that the fiancé was already called husband and could release himself only by an act of repudiation. It would appear that Joseph's integrity did not only consist in wanting to withhold his name from a child he did not know but also, since he was convinced of Mary's virtue, in refusing to expose, to the rigour of the Law, a mystery he did not understand. Immanuel means "God with us."

The Loggia ends in a pair of carved doors; above them is a lunette showing, again, the arms of Leo X, upheld by *putti*.

APPENDIX

(Pages 166, 167) There is a break in the narrative here from the construction of the I
Tabernacle and of the Ark (Exodus 36) through the books of Leviticus and Numbers
until the disobedience of Moses in the second episode of drawing water from the rock
(Numbers 20) and his death (Deuteronomy 32 and 34).

Among the chief events not included are: Rules and regulations, including the Day
of Atonement (Leviticus); the numbering of the Israelites (Numbers 1); ordination
of the Levites as the priestly clan (Ibid.:9); Aaron's rod sprouts (Ibid.:17); the plague
of serpents among the disobedient Israelites and Moses's cure of it with the brazen
serpent (Ibid.:21); the story of Balaam's ass (Ibid.:21).

(Page 182) Another long gap in the sequence of paintings leaves out the death of II
Joshua and the reigns of the Judges. It omits all mention of Gideon, of Samson, and

the moving story of Ruth. These are too long to be told in this narrative, which leads on to the birth of Samuel (I Kings 1).

III   (Pages 197, 201) There is again a long gap, leaving out many of the most interesting events in David's life: his love for Jonathan and his pact with him; his marriage to Saul's daughter; his sparing of Saul's life after Saul's pursuit of him; David's marriage to Abigail; the witch of Endor; the deaths of Samuel, Saul, and Jonathan; and, after David was anointed King, the bringing of the Ark to Jerusalem.

    Omitted, too, are the dramatic revolt of Absalom against his father, David's flight from Jerusalem, and Absalom's death, caught in the branches of an oak tree while riding his mule; the mule left him hanging there and David's men killed him. In spite of his treachery, David mourned him, weeping, "My son Absalom! Absalom, my son, my son! Would to God I had died instead of thee." But David still went from triumph to triumph, and no enemy prevailed over him.